Danger on the Air

A thin stream of liquid was pouring down from the TV studio ceiling and puddling on the floor. The puddle was already beginning to overflow in the direction of the set.

"Gasoline!" said Frank. "It smells like gasoline!"

"We've got to stop the show!" shouted Joe. "It's the Masked Marauder! He must have—"

Before Joe could finish his sentence, there was a sharp explosion overhead. A column of flame rushed down from the ceiling, traveling along the stream of gasoline.

Then the floor of the studio burst into bright orange flames!

The Hardy Boys Mystery Stories

Available from MINSTREL Books

The HARDY BOYS®

DANGER ON THE AIR

FRANKLIN W. DIXON

A MINSTREL® BOOK

PUBLISHED BY POCKET BOOKS

New York   London   Toronto   Sydney   Tokyo

A MINSTREL PAPERBACK *ORIGINAL*

 A Minstrel Book, published by
POCKET BOOKS, a division of Simon & Schuster Inc.
1230 Avenue of the Americas, New York, NY 10020

ISBN: 0-671-66305-4

First Minstrel Books printing April 1989

10 9 8 7 6 5 4 3 2 1

Contents

DANGER
ON THE AIR

1 A Star Is Born

"I'm going to be a star!" crowed Joe Hardy, sitting next to his brother, Frank, in the front seat of their modified police van. "My name up in lights! My face on the covers of magazines!"

Frank Hardy, his hands tight on the steering wheel, glanced at his brother out of the corner of one eye. For fifteen minutes, Joe had been chattering like a cassette tape stuck on fast forward, and Frank was beginning to wonder if he was ever going to slow down.

"Sure," Frank agreed. "*Psychology Today*. You can be Psycho of the Month."

"It'll be a whole new career for me," said Joe, ignoring his brother's sarcasm. "Movies. TV shows. Hollywood, here I come!"

"Let's get to downtown Bayport first," suggested Frank. "We're just going on a TV talk show, not auditioning for a movie."

"Maybe a famous film director will see me,"

said Joe. "Those guys know star quality when they see it!"

"Which is why they won't be watching you," countered Frank. "Besides, 'Faces and Places' is a local show. Nobody'll see us outside of Bayport."

Joe shook his head in disagreement. "Those big-time directors send talent scouts all over the country looking for guys just like me. You never know who'll be watching."

"Okay, okay!" cried Frank, laughingly admitting defeat. "You're going to be a star. And I'll be the next president of the United States! Stranger things have happened!"

"Yeah," agreed Joe. "For instance, you just drove past the TV station."

Frank glanced out the side window of the van and muttered under his breath. On the far side of the street was a large white building with a neon sign on top spelling out WBPT-TV. Underneath was a second sign reading, "Serving the Bayport area with the finest in television since 1953." Maneuvering the van through a wide U-turn, Frank looped into the TV station's parking lot and pulled the van into an open slot.

The two brothers climbed out of the van, then strode up the wide front walk and through the large glass doors at the front of the building. The oversize lobby was decorated in a style that looked like something out of an old movie, with red velvet chairs, and gold trim on the doors and ceiling. Unfortunately, the red velvet upholstery

2

was beginning to look a little frayed and the gold trim had started to chip and peel.

As the brothers walked in, a dark-haired young woman with a clipboard in her hand looked up at them.

"You must be Frank and Joe Hardy," she said with a smile. "I'm Mona D'Angelo, program director here at WBPT and producer of 'Faces and Places.' For a moment, I was afraid you weren't going to get here. You're just in time for the show."

"We're really sorry about that," apologized Frank. "As we told you on the phone, our van had a flat tire on the way over."

"And my brother left the jack at home in the garage," added Joe. "You wouldn't believe what we had to go through to get another one. Anyway, we're glad to meet you, Ms. D'Angelo."

"Oh, I'm the one who's glad to meet *you*," Mona replied, shaking both brothers' hands in turn. "I've been hearing about you boys for quite a while. You're Bayport's most famous detectives."

"Well," said Frank, with a faint look of embarrassment, "we're actually only *amateur* detectives. Our father, Fenton Hardy, is the real detective in the family."

"Be that as it may," said Mona, "the Hardy boys are local celebrities, and we're very happy to have you on our show. I wish we could chat a bit longer, but it's almost airtime, and 'Faces and

3

Places' is a live program.

"And," she added mysteriously as she turned to lead the brothers out of the lobby, "I'm afraid the crew would rather spend as little time around the station as possible right now."

"Why?" asked Frank. "Don't they like their jobs?"

"Usually," replied Mona, her face clouding over. "But we've, ah, had some problems around here lately. I think they're afraid that something might happen."

"Something might happen?" echoed Joe. "That sounds pretty sinister."

"Oh, it's probably nothing," said Mona. "I shouldn't even have mentioned it. Come on. I'll introduce you to the show's host."

Mona led the brothers down a long hallway and into a large studio, where cameramen pushed television cameras around on rolling dollies. A sign just inside the door identified the room as Studio A. Bright, barrel-shaped spotlights hung from metal beams high overhead, creating a pool of light at one end of the room that contrasted sharply with the gloom that surrounded it. The brothers were immediately struck by how large the studio was, larger than anything they had expected to see in a Bayport television station. There were even several rows of seats where a studio audience could sit, though at the moment barely half of the seats were occupied.

"Wow," said Joe admiringly. "This is pretty impressive."

"Yes," agreed Mona. "This is one of the largest television studios on the East Coast, outside of New York, anyway. There's quite a story behind how it got built, but I'm afraid I don't have time to tell it at the moment."

A short, sandy-haired man with an arm full of electronic equipment walked up to Mona. The producer turned to the Hardys and said, "Frank, Joe, I'd like you to meet Tom Langford. Tom does the lighting and sound for 'Faces and Places.'"

"Glad to meet you," said Langford with a smile. "I have to wire you for sound before we go on the air. If you'll each take one of these clip-on mikes . . ." He gave each of the brothers a small microphone, which he helped them clip to their sweaters. "Just don't trip over the wires and you'll be okay. See you later, Mona."

"Thanks, Tom," said Mona. "Now let me introduce you boys to our host."

At the brightly lit end of the studio was a small set consisting of a rug, several chairs, and a backdrop painted to look like a picture window. In one of the chairs sat a well-tanned, middle-aged man in a blue suit. Mona introduced him as Matt Freeman, the host of "Faces and Places."

"Glad to meet you," said Freeman, a wide but slightly phony-looking smile pasted on his face. "Mona's told me quite a bit about you. Just have a seat. We'll be on the air in a couple of minutes."

5

"I'll leave you boys with Matt," Mona said. "Good luck and have fun." She started to walk away, then stopped and turned back. "Oh— could you stop by my office after the show? I'd like to have a few more words with you."

Frank and Joe agreed that they would stop in to see her. When she was gone, Freeman asked if they had had much previous television experience. When they told him that they had not, he pointed at the large cameras, mounted on dollies, bearing down on them.

"We use a three-camera system here. When you see the red light next to the lens on a camera light up, you'll be on the air. Don't look at the camera, though. Just look at me. That'll seem more natural.

"I'll start out by asking you some questions about your crime-fighting career," Freeman went on. "Then I'll ask you to give the viewers a few tips on how to avoid becoming crime victims. That sound all right?"

"Sure," said Frank. "I guess we know a few things on the subject, though we usually don't become involved until after a crime has happened."

"Then you know a lot more about the subject than the rest of us do," said Freeman reassuringly. "Most people have never been involved in a serious crime and don't want to be. I'm sure our viewers will be interested in anything you have to

6

say. When the camera light comes on, just relax and act naturally. Let me do all the work. You just answer the questions."

Frank stared into the dark half of the studio. The bright lights overhead were blinding, and he couldn't see much except for a television monitor just beyond the set. There was a commercial on the air at the moment. It was advertising a television program Frank had never heard of, called "Mrs. Brody's Boardinghouse." A couple of scenes from the show flashed across the screen. Frank was surprised to see that they were in black and white. Must be an old show, he thought.

Suddenly the studio came to life. The title *Faces and Places* appeared on the television monitor in bright red letters. One of the cameras dollied in toward Freeman's chair. The red light next to the lens flashed on. Freeman turned his smile up to its brightest wattage and looked straight into the camera.

"Good afternoon," he boomed, "and welcome to 'Faces and Places,' the show that introduces you to the people who make news in and around the Bayport area. Today our guests are two brothers who are probably already familiar to many of you. These are no typical teenagers. In addition to being high-school students and local football stars, these young men are very successful detectives. They've solved cases that have left the Bayport police baffled and have helped capture

7

criminals who might otherwise never have been brought to justice. Of course, I'm talking about . . ."

Freeman turned toward the brothers. The camera pulled back to get a full shot of the three of them. ". . . Frank and Joe Hardy, better known simply as the Hardy boys. Frank, Joe, it's great to have you on our program!"

Frank nodded. "It's great to be here, Mr. Freeman," he said politely. Joe nodded his agreement, though Frank noticed that his brother seemed strangely silent.

"You can call me Matt, Frank," said the host. "No need to stand on ceremony. Our program is just an informal little get-together between you, me, and about ten thousand viewers in the Bayport area." Freeman smiled and there was scattered laughter from the small studio audience.

"Ten thousand?" Joe gulped, as though the reality of being on television had just hit him. "Ten thousand viewers?"

"That's, uh, right," said Freeman, casting a worried glance in Joe's direction. "So, how did you boys get into crime-fighting?" he asked, changing the subject.

"Well," Frank answered, "our father is Fenton Hardy, who's a pretty well known detective himself."

"Like father, like sons, eh?" Freeman smiled. "Following in Dad's footsteps?"

8

"I guess you could say that," Frank said. "Actually, we just like the excitement of it. And, of course, we like to help people. If somebody's in trouble, we can't resist helping them get out."

"That's a commendable attitude," agreed Freeman. "If everybody felt that way, it would be a much nicer world. What about you, Joe?" He swiveled his chair to face the younger of the two Hardys. "Do you agree with what Frank has to say?"

A worried look crossed Freeman's face. Frank followed the older man's gaze and saw that his brother was sitting rigid in his chair, with a glazed look in his eyes, like a snake hypnotized by a snake charmer. Frank started with surprise. Was this the same Joe Hardy who had been talking a mile a minute on the trip to the studio?

"Joe?" prompted Freeman. "Do you have anything to say about why you chose to become a detective?"

"Um, well, no," mumbled Joe finally, his eyes staring straight ahead. "Whatever Frank says."

Whatever Frank says? Those were three words that Frank Hardy had never expected to hear from his brother! Frank realized suddenly that his brother was suffering from a case of stage fright to end all cases of stage fright. He was scared stiff! Well, thought Frank, I guess I'll just have to carry this interview by myself.

Freeman, who had apparently realized the same thing, turned back to Frank before asking

9

his next question. "I'm sure you boys must have had some pretty interesting cases. What was the most exciting of all the mysteries you've been involved in, Frank?"

"That's a tough one to answer," said Frank truthfully. "I guess it was probably the time we discovered this ring of smugglers that—"

He never finished the sentence.

His voice was drowned out by the roar of an explosion echoing through the studio. Frank turned toward the sound in time to see a cloud of debris come flying out of the back of the room, followed by a foul-smelling puff of smoke.

Frank and Joe automatically threw themselves to the floor, putting the chairs between themselves and the flying debris. Freeman followed a second later, falling to the floor next to Frank. Throughout the studio, there was the sound of technicians and audience members ducking for cover.

Slowly, the echoes of the explosion died away. Frank and Joe peered cautiously over the tops of their chairs, into the rapidly settling cloud of smoke. In the rear of the studio, several small pieces of equipment lay scattered about, and there was a gaping crack in the concrete wall. No one seemed to be hurt, however.

Suddenly a voice cried out: "Help! I'm falling!"

Looking up, Frank and Joe saw that one of the metal beams underneath the high ceiling had been knocked loose by the explosion and was

10

dangling at an odd angle. Halfway along the beam, next to one of the barrel-shaped spotlights, Tom Langford was hanging by one arm.

Even as they watched, the technician's hand began to slip. Within seconds, he was going to fall to the floor—twenty feet below!

2 A New Line of Work

Joe, who had been paralyzed with stage fright only seconds before, suddenly came back to life. He whipped off his microphone, vaulted over the back of his chair, and ran toward a metal ladder attached to the back wall of the studio. Frank hurried after him, but Joe was practically at the top of the ladder before Frank reached the bottom.

About six feet below the ceiling, a metal catwalk ran from one side of the studio to the other. Joe clambered from the ladder to the catwalk and raced to a spot next to where Langford was hanging precariously from the metal beam.

"Here," he said, thrusting one arm out to the dangling man. "Grab my hand. I'll help you reach the catwalk."

The hapless technician did as Joe asked. Joe hooked his feet securely on the far edge of the catwalk and pulled Langford toward him. The

12

damaged beam swayed as the technician's weight shifted. Then it broke away from the ceiling and plummeted to the floor with a resounding crash.

Langford let go of the beam just as it gave way. For a split second he hung in midair with only Joe's tight grip keeping him from falling, then he grabbed the edge of the catwalk. With Joe's help he climbed over the side. A moment later, the two of them had made their way back down the ladder to the studio floor.

"Are you okay?" Joe asked the trembling technician.

"I—I think so," Langford stammered. "Thanks for helping me up there. I'd be in pretty bad shape now if you hadn't."

"That was a close one," said Frank, coming up behind the pair. "How'd you get stuck up there in the first place?"

"Well," said Langford, "I'd gone up to adjust one of the lights and—" Before he could finish the sentence, Mona appeared and beckoned the brothers toward the side door of the studio.

"Follow me," she said. "We're evacuating the building until we find the cause of the explosion. There's a commercial running now. We're going to do the rest of the show from the parking lot."

"The parking lot?" said Joe in astonishment.

"You're actually going to stay on the air after *that*?" asked Frank. "Why don't you just rerun an old situation comedy or something?"

"The show must go on," said Mona, as she led

them out of the building. "Besides, we can't afford not to finish it. 'Faces and Places' is the best-rated show WBPT has, and we've sold all the advertising time. If we don't run the ads, there'll be a lot of trouble with certain individuals in station management who shall remain nameless. Besides, this is the most exciting thing to happen on 'Faces and Places' since we came on the air!"

In the parking lot, Matt Freeman waved them toward an impromptu set constructed from folding chairs. A pair of cameramen stood nearby with handheld cameras. As the brothers approached, a glowing red light appeared on the camera that was pointing toward them. Mona wasn't kidding, they realized. They were still on the air!

"Joe, Frank," Freeman said. "What you did in there was tremendous! An incredible rescue! I want you to tell our viewers all about it!"

The two brothers walked onto the set and numbly took their seats, amazed at the resourcefulness of the production crew and still a little stunned by the explosion. Freeman handed the brothers their microphones and clapped Joe on the back, his broad smile looking a great deal more genuine than it had earlier.

"You're a hero, Joe!" he exclaimed. "Now I see why the Hardy boys have such a fantastic reputation!"

He turned back to the camera. "Ladies and

gentlemen," he intoned to the unseen audience, "as you've just witnessed, there has been some kind of explosion in our Bayport studios. We've evacuated the building but remained on the air, so that those of you at home can stay abreast of events as they happen.

"Perhaps the most incredible of this afternoon's events has been the rescue of one of our station technicians by young Joe Hardy, which you just saw live—"

"Just . . . *saw?*" stammered Joe incredulously. "You mean . . . all of that was on television?"

"Of course," Freeman told him. "We left the cameras running the entire time. Our producer told me on the way to the parking lot that the television networks are already calling for copies of the tape. You're a national hero, son!"

"National hero?" Joe repeated, a stunned look on his face. Uh-oh, thought Frank. Is Joe about to go through another bout of stage fright?

Then he saw a glow of confidence come into Joe's face. "It was nothing," the younger Hardy said modestly. "I just did what anybody else would do. I couldn't let that poor guy fall to the floor. I'm sure Frank would have saved him if I hadn't gotten there first. . . ."

The rest of the show belonged to Joe Hardy. He described in detail what it had felt like to rescue the luckless Langford. Then, at Freeman's urging, he related his entire autobiography, from his first case as a detective to the last touchdown pass

15

he had caught on the football field. Frank found, to his chagrin, that he couldn't get a word in edgewise. He was almost grateful when the show was over.

After the program, Mona reappeared and invited the brothers to join her in her office. "The police bomb squad showed up just after we left the building," she told them. "They're examining the studio now to see if they can find what caused the explosion. I'm told that it's safe to go back inside."

She led them to a corridor that they hadn't seen before, into a suite of offices. Compared to the studio from which 'Faces and Places' was broadcast, Mona's office was a mere cubbyhole, though it was spacious enough to hold Frank, Joe, Mona, and a cluttered desk. The producer motioned for the Hardys to have a seat, then settled down behind the desk herself.

"I enjoyed your interview," she told them. "It was one of our best shows."

"Thanks," said Frank. "The explosion probably helped."

"It did make for an exciting show," agreed Mona. "But you boys are quite articulate. And I was quite impressed by your dramatic rescue, Joe.

"But let me get to the point. I'd like to ask for your help. I mentioned before that we've been having some problems here at WBPT. Well, you got a look at those problems right in the middle of your interview. I guess maybe they're a little bigger than I thought they were."

"You mean the explosion?" asked Joe.

"That's right. I'm rather ashamed to admit that we had some advance warning that an explosion might take place. We called the police, but they found nothing. So we pretty much dismissed the possibility of danger."

"I don't understand," said Frank. "How did you know that something was going to happen?"

"We received a warning," Mona repeated, pulling a small package from her desk. "Here. Take a look at this."

Frank took the package and examined it. It was wrapped in a brown mailing envelope and addressed to the WBPT studios. Inside was a plain black videotape cassette, the same type that the Hardys used on their home VCR. The tape was unmarked.

"What's on the tape?" he asked Mona.

"I'll show you," she said, taking it from his hands. Perched at one end of her cluttered desk was a small portable TV on top of a miniature VCR. She plugged the tape into the appropriate slot and pressed a few buttons. A picture appeared on the screen.

At first the image was mostly static, a bright soup of colored dots. Then a picture appeared: a man—or perhaps a woman—wearing a black

17

leather mask, the sort that a professional wrestler might wear. He or she was staring directly at the viewer.

"Is this some kind of a joke?" Joe asked.

"That's what we thought at first," said Mona. "But I think what happened this afternoon proves that it isn't."

Suddenly the person wearing the mask began to speak. The voice had a strange electronic whine to it, as though it had been filtered through a computer before it was recorded.

"Greetings, friends and neighbors at television station WBPT," said the person behind the mask, in cheerful tones. "This is the Masked Marauder speaking."

"The Masked Marauder?" said Frank unbelievingly. "This must be a joke!"

"Keep listening," cautioned Mona.

"In the spirit of friendly cooperation," the Marauder continued, "I'd like to offer a warning to the staff and on-air personalities at your station. A bomb has been planted somewhere on your premises. Don't bother looking for it; you'll never find it. In a few days, it's going to go off, and there's nothing you can do about it."

"'Friendly cooperation,' huh?" Joe snorted. "This guy's about as friendly as a scorpion."

"You'll hear from me again after the explosion," the Marauder said. "At that time, I'll tell you how you can buy yourself protection from future, ah, accidents. Until then, have a nice

18

day!" The image of the Marauder disappeared, and the colored static returned. Mona pressed another button, and the TV set went dark.

"Sounds like extortion to me," said Frank. "The old protection racket. Do what he asks or he'll blow up the station."

"Exactly," said Mona, "except that he never said what it is he wants. Now that the explosion has taken place, I assume that we'll hear from him again."

"Have you shown this tape to the police?" asked Joe.

"Oh, yes," said Mona. "They've analyzed it quite thoroughly. No fingerprints. No way to trace the tape cassette to the store at which it was purchased. And he's done some sort of electronic thing to his voice so that nobody can make a voiceprint of it. They also searched the studio for a bomb and, as I said, found nothing. Whoever the Marauder is, he's quite clever."

"Now I know why your crew wants to spend less time around the studio," said Joe. "Does everybody here know about this?"

"Probably," said Mona. "We haven't exactly publicized the Marauder's threats, but rumors spread quickly at a TV station. When the tape arrived, of course, we didn't realize what it was, and several people had seen it before we could clamp a lid on it."

"How can we help?" asked Frank.

"I'd appreciate it if you could hang around the

19

station for a while, watch for any suspicious activity, get to know some of the personnel. You'd be a lot less conspicuous than the police, and you have quite a reputation for catching slippery criminals."

"Do you think the Marauder might be someone who works here?" asked Joe.

"It's possible," Mona told him. "I really have no idea. Maybe the Marauder's a disgruntled ex-employee. Or somebody who's taken an irrational dislike to this station."

"Or just somebody who wants money and doesn't care who he hurts while getting it," volunteered Frank.

"Right," said Mona. "So, would you like the job?"

Frank looked at Joe. "Well, we don't have anything else really pressing."

"And it sounds like a pretty interesting case," said Joe.

"I thought you'd think so," said Mona. "I have an offer that might make it even more appealing to you."

She leaned back for a moment and gazed levelly across her desk at the Hardys. "How'd you like to have your own television show?" she asked.

3 Showdown in Studio A

Both Frank and Joe gaped at Mona in astonishment. "Our own television show?" asked Frank.

"Wow!" exclaimed Joe. "I didn't think we were *that* good!"

"Well," said Mona, "I'm exaggerating a little. It wouldn't exactly be your own show. Actually, it would be a daily five-minute spot on 'Faces and Places.' You could give tips to the viewers, tell them how to protect themselves from burglars, muggers, that sort of thing. We could call your segment 'Crimestoppers, Inc.'"

"I'll have to talk to my agent first," joked Frank. "I'll also have to apologize to my brother. He told me that our interview was going to make him a star, and I didn't believe him."

Mona laughed. "I don't know if this is going to make you into stars, exactly. But you will be better known around Bayport than ever before. And"—Mona laced her hands together under

21

her chin—"it'll give you a good excuse for hanging around the studios, watching for our friend the Masked Marauder."

"Ah," said Joe. "An ulterior motive!"

"Quite right," Mona replied with a grin. "But I also think you'd be very good and that the Crimestoppers spot could help our ratings. So what do you say? Will you do the show?"

"It's all right with me if it's all right with my brother," said Frank.

"All right?" said Joe, practically shouting with excitement. "It's terrific! I think I've finally found my place in life—TV star! I guess it was inevitable!"

"When do you want us to start?" asked Frank. "In a couple of weeks? Next month?"

"Uh, how about day after tomorrow?"

Joe stopped celebrating. "Pretty short notice," he said.

"I guess the Masked Marauder won't wait," said Frank. "You'll probably be hearing from him again any day now."

"I'm afraid so," said Mona. "Ordinarily, I'd give you a little more time to prepare for the show, but I'm afraid this will be a rush job. Today is Monday. Do you think you can have a five-minute Crimestoppers spot ready by Wednesday?"

Frank shrugged. "I suppose so. We'll need somebody to show us the ropes around the studio, though."

"I know just the person," said Mona. "I'll introduce you to him tomorrow. Can you be here at eight-thirty in the morning?"

"Sure," said Joe. "I might even be able to drag my sleepyhead brother here with me."

"Hey," responded Frank good-naturedly. "If anybody has to drag anybody—"

There was a knock at the door. The brothers and Mona looked up to see Officer Con Riley standing outside. Con was the boys' friend on the Bayport police force, and he gave them a wink as he came into the office.

"Yes, officer?" asked Mona. "Have you found out what caused the explosion in the studio yet?"

"We think so, ma'am," Con said. "If you don't mind, we'd like the three of you to drop by the studio and answer some questions. Nothing major. Shouldn't take more than a few minutes."

Con, the Hardys, and Mona walked to the studio, where a team of detectives was examining the debris left by the explosion. Some twisted pieces of metal were laid out on the floor, and a forensics expert was dusting them for fingerprints.

"It was a bomb, all right," Con told them. "It may have been a dud, though."

"A dud?" said Joe. "It didn't sound like a dud from where we were sitting."

"It was probably intended to do even worse damage than it did," Con Riley said. "You were very lucky."

"I'll remember that when a *real* disaster strikes," said Mona with a sigh. "Where *was* the bomb, anyway?"

"It's hard to tell exactly," said Con. "The explosion appears to have taken place near the ceiling, probably not far from that broken beam, but there's no way to pin it down exactly. The trouble with bombs is they tend to destroy their own evidence. But maybe the lab boys will turn up something."

The police had already seen the studio tape of the explosion, so their questions were brief. When the interrogation was over, a stocky, balding man stormed into the room, the stub of a cigar clenched between his lips. He glared angrily at the damage from the explosion, then scowled at Mona and the Hardys as though they had somehow been responsible.

"So you're the Hardy brothers?" he growled, flicking cigar ashes into the air. "You don't look like detectives to me."

Frank and Joe turned to Mona and gave her a who-is-this-guy? look.

"I'd like to introduce you boys to our station manager, Bill Amberson," Mona said. "I told Bill that I'd be asking you to hang around the station, keeping an eye out for the Masked Marauder."

"And I told her that I thought it was a lousy idea," snapped Amberson. "Only she didn't have any better suggestions, so I told her to go ahead.

24

These cops sure aren't helping much. I guess you kids can't be any worse."

He turned to glare at a police lab technician who was dismantling one of the lighting fixtures. "Be careful with that!" he shouted, storming off in pursuit of the technician. "Those things cost money!"

"Boy, he's a real charmer!" said Joe, as soon as Amberson was out of earshot.

"Good thing you caught him in a cheerful mood," said Mona. "Actually, he's not a bad guy. A little gruff, but he cares a lot about the station. You should see him when he's *really* angry."

"No thanks," said Frank. "Listen, do you mind if we take a look around the studio? It couldn't hurt to get acquainted with the place, and maybe we can find a few clues."

"It's fine with me," said Mona. "As long as it's all right with the police."

"It ought to be," said Joe. "They seem to be finishing up."

"Then go ahead and look around. You've got the free run of the place. I'll be nearby. Shout if you need me."

"You bet," said Frank, as Mona wandered off to talk to the police.

"What next?" asked Joe. "Now that we're celebrities, we've got to live up to our reputations as hotshot detectives. Got any ideas?"

"Maybe we should try to figure out how the

Marauder got the bomb in here in the first place," suggested Frank. "Do you suppose they let just anybody walk into this studio?"

"I doubt it," said Joe. "I saw a security guard outside the door when we came in with Mona."

"So it was probably somebody the guard already knew."

"Or somebody who slipped past when the guard wasn't looking."

"Maybe," said Frank. He frowned in thought. "Think we should get a list of everybody who came into the studio in the last few days?"

"I don't know if that's a good idea," said Joe. "Even if the guard could remember all the names, I bet we'd get a list as long as your arm. 'Faces and Places' isn't the only show they do in this studio. Check out the stuff they've got against that wall."

Frank looked where his brother was pointing. Stacked against one wall of the studio were about half a dozen painted backdrops from other TV shows. One of them featured a banner reading WBPT News Center. Another depicted a rising sun behind a field of flowers. Joe reached out and lifted one of the light canvas backdrops from the stack.

"What do they make these flats out of?" he asked. "Tissue paper and balsa wood?"

"They sure don't look like they do on television," Frank said. "Just painted canvas in a wood frame."

26

"Hey! What's this?" asked Joe. "Look! Behind these backdrops!"

He pulled the backdrops away from the wall, revealing an open door leading into a darkened hallway.

"Must be a back entrance," Frank said. "Do you think our friend the Masked Marauder might have come in this way?"

"Could be," Joe said. "Shhh!" He waved a hand to tell his brother to be quiet. "I think I see somebody back there."

Frank moved closer to the door, peering into the darkness. "Where? All I see are shadows."

"I saw something move," Joe whispered. "Here. Hold these flats. I'm going to take a closer look."

Frank pulled the surprisingly light pile of backdrops away from the wall, and Joe slipped through the door. The hallway wasn't completely dark, but it was full of weird shadows and dark racks of props and equipment.

This must be where they keep their old sets, thought Joe, edging past stacks of sagging backdrops and old chairs. One end of the hall was a dead end. Joe walked into the shadows, looking for signs of an intruder.

Suddenly he heard the sound of footsteps coming from behind him. Joe turned just in time to see a broad-shouldered figure leap at him— and tackle him around the waist!

27

4 Hero's Welcome

"Hey!"

Joe's cry was cut short as the mysterious figure slammed him back against a wall, taking his breath away. Joe brought up his knee sharply and caught the intruder on the shoulder, knocking him backward. He caught a brief glimpse of a man's face, topped with curly blond hair. The intruder recovered instantly and plunged at Joe a second time. Within seconds, they had wrestled each other to the floor.

"Frank! Mona!" shouted Joe. "I've caught the Marauder!"

"What do you mean, *you've* caught the Marauder!" the intruder bellowed. "*I've* caught the Marauder! Somebody help me!"

There was a burst of noise from the studio as Frank and then Mona rushed into the hallway.

"Let go of my brother!" shouted Frank, grab-

28

bing the mysterious figure from behind and pulling him away from Joe.

"Your brother?" Joe's opponent whirled around. "There are two of you?"

"What in the world is going on here?" asked Mona. "Frank! That's not the Marauder! Let him go!"

Joe stumbled back to his feet, wiping the dust off his sleeves. "I caught this guy snooping around back here," he told the others. "If he's not the Marauder, what's he doing in this dark hallway?"

"I've got the same question about you," said the intruder, as Frank released his grip on him. "I was back here looking for the guy who planted that bomb in the studio." He turned to Mona. "I figured if I found your Masked Marauder for you, it might give me a little more leverage in our discussions."

"Discussions?" asked Frank. "What discussions?"

"Never mind," said Mona. "Frank, Joe, this is Wayne Clintock. We'd appreciate it if you didn't rough him up *too* much."

"Wayne Clintock?" echoed Joe, staring at the tall, broad-shouldered figure in front of him. "*The* Wayne Clintock? I thought you looked familiar. You're the actor, right?"

"Sure," said Frank, staring at the figure in amazement. "You played the mysterious gunman in *Beat the Hangman.*"

"And the sergeant in *Drop Zone: Danger,*" added Joe.

"And the tough cop in *Hogan's Law,*" chimed in Frank.

"I've seen all your movies!" said Joe with a grin. "I'm one of your biggest fans!"

"Me, too!" agreed Frank. "I can't believe this! You're really Wayne Clintock! Wait'll I tell my girlfriend—"

"And Chet Morton!" said Joe.

"And Aunt Gertrude!" said Frank.

"Well," said the hulking Clintock, clearing his throat, "I guess you kids can't be too bad. Better not hang around in any more dark hallways, though. You vouch for these kids, Mona?"

"They've got my seal of approval, Wayne. I guess you haven't heard of the Hardy boys out in California, but here in Bayport these young men are considered top-notch detectives."

"Detectives, eh? Well, I wish you boys luck. If you catch this punk who calls himself the Masked Marauder, tell him he's lucky that Wayne Clintock didn't get his hands on him. You know what I'd do if I caught a punk like that?"

"You bet!" said Joe. "I saw what you did to that gang of thugs in *War in the Streets*—"

"—and to the terrorists in *The Last Blast,*" said Frank.

"Well," said Clintock, with his trademark drawl, "that's what I'd do to this Masked Marauder fella."

30

"Wow!" said Joe. "It's a good thing Mona was here to tell you that *I* wasn't the Masked Marauder."

"Looks that way," said Mona drily. "Listen, boys, it's late in the afternoon and I'm sure Mr. Clintock wants to get back to his hotel room. You'll have another chance to talk to him on Wednesday, when you do your first Crimestoppers spot on 'Faces and Places.' Mr. Clintock has agreed to be our featured guest on the show that afternoon."

"That's terrific!" said Frank. "Uh, do you think I could get your autograph? For my girlfriend, of course," he added with a touch of embarrassment.

"Yeah," said Joe. "I'd like one, too. To give to my aunt Gertrude, I mean."

"No problem, boys," said Clintock. "Always glad to do a favor for my fellow lawmen."

"'Fellow lawmen,'" repeated Joe. "I like the sound of that."

After they left the studio, Frank and Joe headed for the Bayport Mall and Mr. Pizza. "Looks like the whole gang is here," said Frank as they walked in. "There's Callie—"

"And Iola," cried Joe, waving toward a table halfway across the room. "Come on. Let's tell them about Wayne Clintock!"

Callie Shaw, an attractive girl with blond hair and brown eyes, stood and waved at the brothers.

Callie was Frank's girlfriend. Sitting at the table next to her was Iola Morton, Joe's girlfriend, a dark-eyed brunette.

"Joe!" shouted Iola, jumping to her feet. "We saw you on television. It was so brave the way you rescued that poor man after the explosion!"

"Guess who we just met," Frank said enthusiastically. "Wayne—"

"Never mind that," Callie cut him off. "Joe, you're a hero! Everybody saw what you did on that show!"

"Um, they did?" said Joe.

"They sure did!" said Iola. "The whole town's talking about it. I'm so proud of you."

"Hey!" said a familiar voice from the back of the room. "If it isn't He-Man Hardy, Free-lance Hero." Chet Morton came toward the brothers, a smirk on his broad face. Chet, a heavyset teenager who played on the high school football team with the Hardys, was Iola's brother and an old friend of Frank and Joe's.

"I expect to see your face on the front page of tomorrow's paper, Joe." Chet laughed. "The headline will read, 'Miracle Occurs! Joe Hardy Rescues Falling Man Without Tripping Over His Own Shoelaces!'"

Joe blushed. "Cut it out, Chet. I just did what you would have done under the circumstances."

"Excuse me," said a voice from a nearby table. Joe turned to see a middle-aged man sitting with his family around the remains of a large pizza.

The man smiled at Joe and said, "I couldn't help noticing—aren't you the young man who was on that TV show this afternoon? 'Faces and Places'?"

"Uh, yes," said Joe.

"My whole family was watching the show. We were really quite impressed with what you did. Would it be possible for us to get your autograph?"

"My *autograph*?" asked Joe in astonishment.

"I don't believe this!" said Chet. "You actually want Joe Hardy's autograph?"

"This young fellow is a genuine hero," said the man. "You shouldn't make fun of that."

Suddenly there was a commotion in the room as dozens of heads swiveled toward the Hardys. "That's Joe Hardy!" somebody murmured. "The guy who was on that show?" somebody else asked. "Wow! He's really cute!" said a female voice. "And he has guts!" added another.

All at once Joe found himself surrounded by people he had never met before, asking for his autograph. Not all of them had seen "Faces and Places" that afternoon, but there didn't seem to be a person in the room who hadn't at least heard about it. As Joe signed his name on paper napkins and school notebooks, Frank looked on with amusement, completely ignored. Even when the last autograph had been signed, the crowd still hung around, asking Joe questions about the explosion and his daring rescue. Finally, Joe gave

33

his brother a desperate look and whispered, "Get me out of this place!"

"Sorry, folks, but our aunt Gertrude was expecting us home an hour ago," Frank announced. "Joe and I have to be running." He grabbed his brother's arm and pulled him out the door of the pizza parlor.

"That was embarrassing," Joe said, once they were outside. "Chet Morton'll be making fun of me for the rest of my life."

"Chet's outnumbered now," Frank said. "And, remember, you heroes have a duty to your admiring public. Better get used to it."

"Yeah, well, it's going to take some work."

"Just this afternoon, you were telling me how you were going to be a star," Frank reminded his brother.

"Did I say that?" Joe asked in astonishment.

Bright and early the next morning, the Hardys drove to the WBPT studios. When they arrived, Mona was waiting for them in her office. She accompanied them to Studio A, where she introduced them to the young man who would serve as their guide into the world of television production.

"This is Johnny Berridge," she told them. "He's the head cameraman on 'Faces and Places.' I've asked Johnny to show you around, help you get started with your Crimestoppers, Inc. segments. If you've got any questions, don't hesitate to ask Johnny, okay?"

Berridge was an open-faced young man in his midtwenties, with bright red hair and an engaging grin. He shook hands enthusiastically with Frank and Joe and told them that they were free to ask him for help on any problems they might encounter in putting together their "show." Mona then excused herself and went back to her office.

"The thing you have to remember about television," Berridge told the brothers, "is that it's mostly illusion. All you need is a couple of props and a good imagination. The rest takes care of itself."

"Yeah," said Joe. "We saw that pile of painted flats in the back of the studio."

"Pretty flimsy, aren't they?" Berridge laughed. "And yet when they appear on camera, they look like expensive movie sets. That's the magic of video."

"What sort of set will we be using for Crimestoppers, Inc.?" asked Frank.

"Probably just a table and a blue backdrop," said Berridge. "We'll go into the prop shop this afternoon and see if we can find some small props that you can use. And I'll have somebody whip up a slide with the words *Crimestoppers, Inc.* on it so we can chroma-key it behind you while you're on the air."

"Chroma-key?" asked Joe, a baffled look on his face.

"Another of our video magic tricks," Berridge said. "I'll tell you more about it in a minute. Listen, wait here while I get my equipment and we'll do a brief rehearsal." The energetic young cameraman disappeared through the door of a nearby room before the Hardys could say another word.

"I hope being a TV star is as easy as he makes it sound," said Frank.

"Me, too," agreed Joe. "I just—"

Joe's voice was drowned out by a shout from the room where Berridge had just gone, followed by a loud clattering noise. Suspecting trouble, the brothers raced through the door of the equipment room that Berridge had entered.

The cameraman was lying on the floor, not moving, in a pool of glistening liquid. A sharp odor filled the air. A metal can lay next to Berridge's shoulder.

"Gasoline!" Joe shouted in horror.

5 The Masked Marauder Strikes Again

"Are you okay?" Frank asked, shaking Berridge's shoulder.

The cameraman groaned and nodded his head. "Yeah," he said, sitting up slowly. "Just a little stunned."

"What happened?" Joe asked. "Did someone attack you?"

"Y-yeah, sort of," Berridge replied shakily, looking around. "When I walked in here, I saw somebody dart behind that rack. I called out, and he threw something at me—that gasoline can, I guess. It hit me in the head. I must have been unconscious for a few seconds."

"The Marauder!" said Joe. "I'll bet he was getting ready to start a fire!"

"Did you get a look at him?" asked Frank.

"No. I'm not even sure if it was a man or a woman. He—the Marauder—was wearing a black mask. And a green army fatigue jacket, like

37

you can buy at surplus stores. That's all I noticed before the can came flying at me."

"Did you see where the Marauder went?" asked Joe.

"Probably through there," said Berridge, pointing toward the back of the equipment room. "If he'd gone out the front way, you guys would have seen him."

Frank found a door in the back of the room and pushed it open. He looked down the hallway outside. "Nobody back here," he said. "He's probably clear out of the station by now."

Joe helped Berridge to his feet. "Listen," said Berridge, "I'd better go change clothes before I finish showing you guys around. I smell like I've been hanging around a gas station all day."

"Do you still feel like giving us the grand tour?" asked Frank.

"Sure," said Berridge. "I was just a little shaken up after getting knocked on the head. I'll be back in a second."

Berridge vanished into the studio. Frank pulled a handkerchief from his pocket and used it to pick up the gasoline can, gingerly examining it.

"We'd better give this to the police," he said to his brother. "There might be fingerprints on it."

"I'll bet they don't find any," Joe said. "This Marauder guy's too smart."

"Yeah, but we'd better go through the formalities. You never know when he might make a mistake."

Berridge came back a few minutes later, wearing a fresh pair of jeans and a red T-shirt with the WBPT logo on it. "I always keep a change of clothes in my locker," he explained. "Sometimes I'm here all night working on special projects, and it's nice to slip into something clean the next morning."

"We were going to rehearse our Crimestoppers spot?" prompted Frank.

"We can get to that later," said Berridge. "I want to get somebody to clean up this gasoline first. In the meantime, I'll introduce you to some of the staff."

Berridge led them back into the studio, where he introduced Frank and Joe to a couple of cameramen who were standing around checking their equipment. Then he went off to find someone to clean up the equipment room.

When Berridge returned, he led the Hardys down a short hallway and into a small room packed with electronic gear that looked as if it belonged on the bridge of a spaceship. Four television monitors stared down from the wall. Three of them showed Studio A as viewed through the cameras inside. The fourth was displaying the show that was currently being broadcast, a prerecorded soap opera. Underneath the fourth monitor was a plate reading On Air.

"This is the director's booth," said Berridge. He nodded at a small, sandy-haired man perched over a console covered with buttons and dials. "I think you've already met Tom Langford. Tom, these are the Hardy boys."

"I know," said the sandy-haired man, reaching out to clasp Joe's hand. "You saved my life yesterday, Joe. I'm sorry I didn't have a chance to say a proper thank-you."

"That's right," said Frank. "You're the guy who was, uh, hanging from the beams yesterday."

Langford laughed. "I was *almost* the guy squashed flat on the floor yesterday! If it hadn't been for the quick thinking of your brother here, I *would* have been. I can't thank you enough, Joe."

"You don't have to thank me," said Joe. "I was glad to help out."

"Well, I'm sure grateful you did," said Langford.

"Tom is the best all-around engineering and production man at the station," explained Berridge. "He directs our morning news show and does lighting and sound on 'Faces and Places.' He's also our electronic special-effects wizard. Don't ask me when he finds time to sleep."

"Sleep? What's that?" joked Langford.

"Frank and Joe will be doing a five-minute spot on 'Faces and Places,'" Berridge told Langford. "I'm showing them around the studio, getting them acquainted with the way we do things at WBPT."

40

"I've heard a rumor," Langford said to the Hardys, "that you're also looking for the person who planted the bomb in the studio yesterday. The so-called Masked Marauder."

"Word travels fast," said Joe. "Yeah, we've been asked to keep our eyes open. You guys know anybody who might hold a grudge against this station?"

"Sure." Berridge laughed. "Just about everybody who works here!"

"Agreed," said Langford. "I don't know anybody at this station who doesn't feel overworked and underpaid. Old man Amberson is the biggest tightwad since Ebenezer Scrooge, and he's not much fun to work for . . . but I don't know if that's reason enough to blow up the studio."

"And after that last ratings book," said Berridge, "it's not like Amberson has money to burn."

"Ratings book?" asked Frank.

"The report that tells us how many people are watching our shows," explained Berridge. "And not many people are."

"Things aren't going well, huh?" said Frank.

"That's an understatement," said Berridge. "Things haven't gone well at WBPT since the days when Angus McParton tried to start a fourth television network."

"A fourth network?" asked Joe. "You mean like CBS or NBC?"

"Or ABC," Berridge added. "Those three net-

41

works have dominated the television industry since it started in the late 1940s. Even before that, back to the early 1930s, they dominated the radio industry. Angus McParton was a tough-minded Scottish immigrant who came to this country in the early 1920s. Within thirty years he had built up a small fortune, and he used a large hunk of it to start WBPT. He intended for this station to be the flagship of a fourth television network, which he called the McParton Network."

"Is that why you have these big studios?" asked Frank.

"Right," said Berridge. "And all of this state-of-the-art 1953 equipment. But the McParton Network never got off the ground and old Angus was forced to sell the entire operation, except for the WBPT studios. He passed away about ten years ago, but the station is still in the McParton family. In fact, Bill Amberson is his nephew. But the old man never really recovered from the failure of the McParton Network. He had one hit series, but it wasn't enough."

"What was the hit?" asked Joe.

"A situation comedy called 'Mrs. Brody's Boardinghouse.' It was a classic among early television programs, though it's nearly forgotten today."

"Wait a minute!" exclaimed Frank. "I saw an advertisement for 'Mrs. Brody's Boardinghouse' just before we were interviewed on 'Faces and Places' yesterday!"

Berridge broke out in a wide grin. "Yes! Our pride and joy! It was believed for years that no copies of 'Mrs. Brody's Boardinghouse' existed, that the whole series had been lost forever. There was no such thing as videotape in those days and 'Mrs. Brody's Boardinghouse' was broadcast live, from the same studio where we produce 'Faces and Places.'

"But a couple of weeks ago," he went on, "an unexpected cache of kinescopes was found tucked away under a pile of old sets and props from the McParton Network days."

"Kinescopes?" asked Joe.

"Films made directly off a TV monitor. It was the only way to preserve live television shows in the early 1950s. Apparently, somebody went to the trouble of kinescoping *all* of the episodes of 'Mrs. Brody's Boardinghouse,' but I guess they forgot to tell anybody where they were."

"I'll bet you were pretty excited when they were found," said Frank.

"Excited?" said Berridge. "We were ecstatic. In this business, finding early episodes of a classic TV series is like the discovery of King Tut's tomb."

"So what do you plan to do with them?" asked Frank. "Donate them to the Smithsonian?"

"No way," said Berridge. "We're going to show

them. And sell them to other stations around the country so that they can show them, too."

"You're kidding!" said Joe. "Who's going to watch such an old TV series?"

"You might, for one," said Berridge. "It's a very good show, and it's still quite watchable today. It has a major star in it, too."

"A major star?" asked Frank. "Who?"

Berridge smiled enigmatically. "Show them one of the kinescopes, Tom. I think they'll get a kick out of this."

"One episode of 'Mrs. Brody's Boardinghouse,' coming right up." Langford grinned and left the studio. Moments later he came back bearing a large film canister. He pulled a reel of film from the canister and threaded it through a projectorlike device in the rear of the director's booth.

"I'll patch it through the on-air monitor," said Langford, punching some buttons on the console. The projector began to chatter, its reels spinning. A fuzzy black-and-white picture replaced the soap opera on the fourth monitor.

"Pretty awful picture," said Joe.

"Yes," said Berridge. "These old kinescopes aren't that great. Makes you grateful for videotape."

The words *Mrs. Brody's Boardinghouse* appeared, accompanied by a tinny musical jingle. Then the names of the stars flashed on the screen.

44

"I don't recognize any of the actors' names," commented Frank.

"Just wait," said Berridge. "You'll see."

The credits faded out, and the image of a large living room appeared. A door opened, and a tall, fat boy entered, a battered lunch pail in his hands and comical black spectacles masking half his face.

"Mrs. Bro-o-o-o-o-o-o-o-dy-y-y-y-y-y-y!" the fat boy called, in a high-pitched nasal whine.

Joe laughed. "What a nerd!" he exclaimed. "Who is this kid, anyway?"

"Take a closer look," suggested Berridge. "Don't you recognize him?"

"Huh?" said Frank. "I've never seen this guy before!"

"Imagine what he'd look like if he were middle-aged and forty pounds lighter. Not easy to do, I admit . . ."

"Wait!" said Joe suddenly. "He *does* look familiar!"

"You're right," said Frank. "Oh, no! That can't be who I *think* it is!"

"Who do you think it is?" asked Berridge.

"Wayne Clintock!" the brothers cried simultaneously.

"Bingo!" said Berridge. "Today's number-one box office attraction, just seventeen years old and starring in his first major role!"

"But I didn't see his name in the credits," Joe said.

"He wasn't using the name Wayne Clintock then. He was going under his real name, Francis Gooch."

"I can't believe that's Wayne Clintock!" Joe said in astonishment. "I'll never be able to look at his movies in the same way again!"

"Me, neither," agreed Frank. "I'm surprised that Clintock is going to let you show this thing."

"If Clintock had his way, we wouldn't. That's why he's flown out here to talk to us. We've offered him a decent sum of money for the rights to the show, which we're not obligated to do under the terms of the contract he signed with the McParton Network, but he'd prefer that these kinescopes stay lost for another hundred years or so. He's right, I suppose. This isn't going to help his macho image any."

"It may turn him into a laughingstock," said Joe. "Why don't you bury these things as a favor to him?"

"To be honest, we need the money. WBPT is having trouble selling advertising time. If we don't come up with something that will bring in decent ratings, we may have to start bankruptcy proceedings within the year. Bill Amberson is betting that we can get pretty good ratings with 'Mrs. Brody's Boardinghouse' on the basis of audience curiosity alone—and pick up a few bucks on the side by syndicating it to other stations."

"But these kinescopes look so awful," said

Frank. "How many people are going to tune in to watch a blurry old black-and-white film shot off a television monitor?"

"We're going to use a little of that video magic I talked about earlier," said Berridge. "Tell them about it, Tom. That's your area of expertise."

"Right," said Langford. "That old skinflint Amberson got so excited when he saw these kinescopes that he went out and bought us a state-of-the-art digital effects board, so that we can process these old kinescopes back onto videotape. We're going to sharpen up the images and even add color to them."

"That sounds pretty expensive," said Joe. "How can a station about to go bankrupt afford to buy a digital effects board?"

"It didn't cost as much as you'd think," said Langford. "It uses the new microchip technology, the same as is used in home computers. You'd be surprised at how cheaply that stuff can be manufactured. The cost wasn't exactly a drop in the bucket, but it was a lot less expensive than you might think. And it's a good investment. If 'Mrs. Brody's Boardinghouse' is a hit, the board will more than pay for itself."

"Show them what you can do with it," suggested Berridge.

"Always happy to strut my stuff," said Langford, rattling the buttons on the console. The projector stopped, and the image on the screen froze. "I can control the effects board

47

directly from this panel," Langford explained. "Watch what the image processor can do."

He turned a knob on the console and the picture seemed to brighten. A ripple passed from the top of the picture to the bottom, and the fuzzy look of the kinescope began to vanish, replaced by a sharp black-and-white image. The ripple passed across the screen a second time, and tiny details began to appear that hadn't been visible before. After the ripple had passed across the screen a third time, the picture looked as sharp as a freshly developed photograph.

"Incredible!" said Frank. "Looks just like new!"

"It's called image enhancement," Langford said. "NASA developed the technique to clean up the pictures sent back from the Voyager space probes. Now watch while I add color to it."

Langford pushed a button and a tiny arrow appeared on the screen. Using a joystick on the console, Langford moved the arrow until it was pointed at Wayne Clintock's face. "I adjust the red, green, and blue levels until I have something approximating flesh tones," said Langford as he twiddled a trio of knobs, "and . . . voilà!" He pushed another button and Clintock's face filled with a rich pink color. Then he pointed the arrow at Clintock's shirt, and within seconds it had been painted a deep blue. A few minutes and a lot of button pushing later, Langford had changed the black-and-white picture on the screen into a color picture.

"That's great!" said Joe. "But do you have to do that on each frame of the film? It'd take you forever to color one episode of the show."

"No problem," said Langford. "At this point, the computer built into the effects board takes over." Langford pressed a button. The projector began rolling again, and the image started moving, this time in slow motion. The fuzzy kinescope image that they had seen a moment before had now been replaced by a sharp color image.

"The computer automatically fills in the color in each frame until the scene changes, then I have to plug in the colors again. Fortunately, the directors on these old shows didn't change scenes very often, so colorizing one of these episodes ought to be a piece of cake."

"Tom will be taking some time off over the next few weeks to colorize and enhance the entire series, so that we can syndicate it," Berridge said. "In the meantime, we'll be showing a few of the old kinescopes on WBPT just to whet the audience's appetite."

"That special-effects board is pretty amazing," said Frank. "Joe, I bet we could use something like that in our detective work. Remember the time we had that film of a bank robbery that was so blurry nobody could make out the robber's face? Think of what we could have done with Tom's help."

"You ain't seen nothing yet," said Langford. "This board has power to spare, and I won't be using more than a fraction of it to spiff up this old series. Watch this!"

Langford spun a knob and the image on the screen expanded until one of the buttons on Wayne Clintock's shirt filled the screen. Then he spun the knob in the opposite direction and the picture shrank, until the entire image was the size of a postage stamp.

"I love it!" said Frank. "It's like a video game!"

With another turn of the knob, Langford started the image of Wayne Clintock spinning rapidly, like a top. When it was spinning so fast that the picture was little more than a blur, Langford brought the image to an abrupt halt. Then he began to distort it, as though the image were drawn on a soft rubber sheet.

"Show them the chroma-key," suggested Berridge.

Langford nodded. As his fingers moved rapidly over the console, the image of Mrs. Brody's boardinghouse living room on the monitor vanished and was replaced by the picture from one of the cameras in Studio A. Two cameramen stood restlessly in the center of the picture, unaware that they were being watched.

"Do you see that blue backdrop behind those two cameramen?" Langford asked.

"Sure," said Joe. "It's hard to miss."

"The special effects board uses a technique

called chroma-keying to replace the blue background with any other background that we want to use. Watch this!"

Langford flicked a switch and the blue background vanished. Suddenly the cameramen were standing in the living room of Mrs. Brody's boardinghouse. Fat young Wayne Clintock sat directly behind one of the oblivious men, chatting with a matronly woman in a polka-dot apron.

Frank laughed. "You didn't tell us that this was a time machine, too!"

"That's the magic of video!" exclaimed Berridge. "I told you Tom was a wizard! Like I said earlier, we'll be using the chroma-key in your Crimestoppers spot to project the slide of a new background with the title of your spot on it. Saves us from having to paint a new set for you."

"I'll never believe anything I see on television again," said Joe.

A sharp knocking interrupted the conversation. Berridge opened the door and a distraught Mona D'Angelo rushed into the director's booth.

"Are you watching the on-air monitor?" she asked breathlessly. "Have you seen what's being broadcast on our station right now?"

"No," said Berridge. "We were showing the boys a few of our special effects tricks."

"Turn it on!" Mona shouted. "You've got to cut him off the air!"

"Cut *who* off the air?" asked Berridge, though Langford was already punching buttons on his

51

console. The studio scene vanished from the monitor and was replaced by the image of a familiar masked face.

"You can call me the Masked Marauder," the image was saying, in a friendly electronic voice. "And I've got an exciting message for WBPT-TV and all of its viewers!"

6 Attack of the Killer Crane

"Where did *he* come from?" shouted Berridge. "How did he get on the air?"

"I don't know," said Langford. "He seems to be on the direct transmitter feed from main engineering. I think I can patch something in over him." Langford looked at the console for a few seconds, then fiddled with some buttons. Finally, the image of the Masked Marauder was replaced by a colorful test pattern.

"Put up the standby slide," said Mona, her voice trembling.

"No problem," said Langford. At the punch of another button, a message reading Please Stand By appeared on the screen.

"Let's get over to main engineering," said Berridge. "If he's in there, maybe we can catch him before he gets away!"

Berridge threw open the door to the director's

53

booth and raced into the hallway, the Hardys, Mona, and Langford directly on his heels. Two doors down, they entered a room that looked like a larger version of the one they had just come from, with electronic equipment lining the walls. The room was unoccupied. There was no sign of the Masked Marauder.

"Here it is!" Berridge cried. A small video cassette recorder was sitting on a table next to a wall-size electronic console. A light on the front panel indicated that the recorder was turned on. A black wire ran from the back of the recorder to a jack on the wall. Berridge pressed the eject button on the recorder, and an unlabeled cassette popped out.

"I'll bet this is from our friend," said Berridge, waving the cassette at the others.

"Amazing!" said Langford. "He patched it directly into the transmitter. It's lucky I was able to override it from the booth. Obviously, this guy knows what he's doing."

"Let's take that cassette to my office," Mona suggested wearily. "I want to see what he has to say."

"No," said a gravelly voice from the doorway. Bill Amberson stepped inside, cigar held aloft in one hand. "We'll take it to *my* office! I want to see what this guy has to say, too . . . and you people had better have a pretty good explanation of how that little message got on the air. Because if you

54

don't, you'll be spending the rest of this week in an unemployment line!"

Amberson's office was about three times as large as Mona's. A projection screen television, about four feet high and five feet wide, sat on one side of the room. On the other side sat Frank, Joe, Mona, Berridge, and Langford. Matt Freeman, who had joined them on the way from main engineering, stood next to the door. Amberson pushed the cassette into a slot on a large VCR next to the projection screen.

"What does this guy *want* from me?" said Amberson to nobody in particular. "It's not like I don't have enough headaches already."

"Maybe he'll tell us what he wants on the tape," Mona suggested.

"Terrific!" growled Amberson. "I can't wait."

He pushed the play button on the VCR and the masked face of the Marauder appeared on the large screen. He smiled at his unseen audience and said, "Good morning, ladies and gentlemen! You've probably heard about the explosion at WBPT yesterday. Maybe you even saw it, if you were watching 'Faces and Places' . . . which is certainly *my* favorite television show."

"With viewers like this, who needs good ratings?" groaned Amberson.

"You can call me the Masked Marauder," the mysterious figure continued. "And I've got an exciting message for WBPT-TV and all of its viewers! In just a little more than twenty-four hours, I'm going to strike again. And this time, somebody might really get hurt! But, since I'm in a generous mood, I'm going to give my friends at WBPT a chance to save their skins. I can be persuaded to change my mind . . . but only with the right inducement.

"If station manager Bill Amberson will check his mail, he'll find a letter from a Mr. M. M. Smith. That's me, Bill! The letter will tell you exactly what I'd like you to do. Read it carefully and do what it says. Or you'll hear from me again . . . tomorrow!"

With a cackling electronic laugh, the Marauder reached out and threw a switch just out of viewing range. His picture was replaced by colored static.

Amberson turned off the VCR and the television. "The mail, eh?" he said. "What's the guy talking about, anyway?"

"Here it is," said Berridge, rummaging through some letters on Amberson's desk. "From a Mr. M. M. Smith. Think that stands for Masked Marauder Smith?"

"What else?" said Amberson, snatching the letter away from Berridge and ripping open the envelope.

"Be careful with the envelope," protested Frank. "There might be fingerprints on it."

"This guy hasn't left fingerprints on anything yet," said Amberson. "I don't see why he'd start now. Oh, this is wonderful! You know what he says in this letter? He wants us to pass him a million dollars in hundred-dollar bills on a street corner in downtown Bayport, or he'll blow up the station. He's out of his mind!"

"Are we going to do it?" asked Mona.

"What?" replied Amberson. "Are you crazy, too? Where are we going to get the million bucks? I don't know if you've heard, but we're a little strapped for cash around here. Maybe we'd be better off if he blew the place up and got it over with."

"At least we can evacuate the station tomorrow to make sure everybody's safe," said Mona.

"No way!" said Amberson, practically biting off the end of his cigar. "We can't afford to close down! It's a good thing you got that tape off the air before he made his threat. I want this whole thing put under wraps. Nobody is to say a word about any of this outside of my office, is that clear? Tomorrow we're going to have business as usual around this place."

"You'll have to tell the police," said Joe. "What that guy is threatening is a felony, and you'd be committing a felony yourself if you tried to cover it up."

"Okay, okay," said Amberson. "We'll tell the police. Maybe they'll supply a few officers to stand guard around the station, so that this Marauder guy can't get in to plant another bomb. But we're not closing down. Is that understood?"

Mona sighed. "Yes, it's understood. But I don't agree with your decision. I think you're taking an unnecessary risk."

"Nobody's asking you to agree with me, young lady. You should be grateful you still have your job after this debacle. And what about you kids?" Amberson snapped, gesturing toward the Hardys. "What good have you done so far?"

"Give them time," said Mona. "I only asked them to help yesterday."

"As a matter of fact, I've got a suggestion," said Frank. "If you don't plan to pay this guy, why not leave an empty briefcase at the street corner where he expects to find the money? The police can keep a watch on the briefcase. If anybody shows up looking for it, they can take him into custody. It might be the Marauder."

"Well," said Amberson, "at least you're using your brain for something besides a hat rack. That's not a bad idea. I'll pass it on to the cops. Maybe one of you kids can go along to help out. Anything else?"

"Maybe you can help *us* a bit," said Joe. "Do you know of anybody who might want to sabotage this station?"

"Try our competition," growled Amberson. "Maybe they don't like the ratings that we get."

"Ha!" Langford laughed. "Our competition *loves* the ratings we get. Or maybe I should say the ratings that we *don't* get!"

"I've got a suggestion," said Matt Freeman. "I'd be willing to bet that our dear Mr. Amberson hasn't told you boys that WBPT may be the victim of a hostile buy-out by a major corporation."

Amberson's eyes flashed angrily. "That's confidential information, Freeman! I told you not to discuss that with anyone else!"

"You've asked these kids to help you, Bill. Maybe you should be honest with them. It doesn't help any of us if you withhold information from them."

"Who's trying to buy the station?" asked Joe.

Amberson leaned back in his chair and stared at the Hardys through half-lidded eyes. "All right," he said with a sigh. "I'll tell you. The buyer is Mediatronics, Inc."

"Mediatronics?" asked Frank. "Aren't they the ones that own the Electronics Attic stores?"

"Right," said Joe. "Those stores where they sell televisions, radios, home computers, that sort of thing?"

"That's the one," said Amberson. "Mediatronics has been trying to buy out WBPT for years, but we've managed to hold them off. They have this crazy idea about starting a fourth television network."

59

"Like Angus McParton?" said Frank.

"Yeah," said Amberson, with the slightest hint of a smile. "Old Uncle Angus. You kids have been doing your homework, haven't you? What they really want is to get their hands on McParton's studios, which they can combine with some of their own electronic equipment to create a home base for the network. They'd fire everybody at the station, of course, myself included."

"So what does that have to do with the Marauder?" Joe asked. "Do you think that Mediatronics wants to blow up the station?"

"Why not?" asked Freeman. "Maybe they're trying to scare us into selling. Or to lower the value of the property, so they can snatch up a bargain."

"But if it's the studios that they want," Frank said, "why would they risk harming them?"

"Maybe it's all a bluff," said Joe. "That bomb yesterday was a dud, according to the police. Maybe there won't be another bomb—or maybe it'll be another dud."

"It might be worth checking out," said Frank. "Where's Mediatronics based?"

"In New York City," said Amberson. "They've got a branch office here in Bayport, but there's nobody worth talking to there. We deal directly with the president, Ettinger, in the corporate offices in New York. You're not thinking of talking with the Mediatronics people, are you?"

"Why not?" said Joe. "You guys asked us to do a little investigating. Do you want us to do it or not?"

"Okay, okay!" snapped Amberson. "Just be careful what you say to them. The negotiations are delicate enough as it is. I don't want those guys ticked off at us."

"It's not quite noon," said Frank. "Maybe I can catch the one o'clock train to New York and have a talk with the folks at Mediatronics."

"I'll stick around here and put our Crimestoppers spot together for tomorrow," said Joe. "And keep my eyes open for the Masked Marauder."

"We've talked enough," said Amberson, rising to his feet. "I don't want you guys discussing any of the stuff we just talked about with anybody outside of this room, understood? I'll handle the cops; you folks just do your jobs. And I want you kids reporting back to me the minute you learn anything about this Masked Marauder jerk."

Outside of Amberson's office, Berridge drew the Hardys aside. "Before you get off on the trail of the Masked Marauder, Frank, I need to know —have you boys decided what you're going to be doing on your Crimestoppers spot tomorrow afternoon?"

"Yeah," said Frank. "We're going to put together a demonstration to show viewers the difference between using a dead bolt and a core lock

61

and how burglars find core locks a lot easier to open."

"All we'll need for the demonstration," said Joe, "is a couple of doors and a couple of locks. Think you've got something like that lying around?"

"You wouldn't believe the stuff we've got lying around here." Berridge laughed. "This building is like a giant storage bin, with old sets and props dating back to the days of Angus McParton. Come on. Before you take off for New York, Frank, you might want to take a glance at the storage area in back of Studio A."

Frank and Joe followed Berridge back down the hallway and into the studio. Once again, they were impressed by the sheer size of Studio A.

"I can see why Mediatronics wants to buy this place," said Frank. "This is practically like a Hollywood studio in here."

"Yeah," said Joe. "What's that old thing there, Johnny? Looks like a small oil derrick."

Berridge laughed. "That's a camera crane. Another leftover from the McParton Network days. The platform on top is where the cameraman sits, for overhead shots of the set. The wheeled carriage on the bottom moves it around the studio. The long arm is used to raise and lower the camera. In the old days, it took about ten technicians to push that thing around the studio, but a few years ago we installed a motor in it. Now we can control it electronically."

62

"Pretty nice," said Frank admiringly. "Hey, did I just see that thing move?"

"Not likely," said Berridge. "We only use it for special shows."

"No!" shouted Joe. "It *is* moving! And it's coming right at us!"

7 Unfriendly Reception

The old camera crane swooped down at the Hardys like a scythe.

"Duck!" Joe shouted, as he and Berridge flattened themselves on the floor.

"You don't have to tell me twice!" cried Frank as he dropped down next to Joe and Berridge. The crane whizzed past a few inches above their heads.

"Whew!" sighed Joe, stumbling back to his feet. "What caused it to do that? There's nobody else in the studio!"

"I—I don't know," stammered Berridge. "It's—"

"Heads up!" shouted Frank. "It's coming back!"

The crane had creaked to a halt and now was swinging back in the opposite direction. The wheels on the crane platform began to spin, and the crane seemed to race straight toward the trio.

64

"It's gone haywire!" shouted Joe, leaping out of the way of the swinging crane. He turned and cast a desperate glance at the wall behind him. They were trapped in a corner of the studio!

"Where are the controls on that thing?" Frank asked Berridge urgently. "At the base, near the wheels?"

"N-no! They're on the platform at the top, where the cameraman sits!"

"Look out," cried Joe. "Here it comes again!"

As the crane swung at them a third time, Frank leaped into the air and landed on the uppermost section.

"Oof!" he groaned. "I've got it!"

"Terrific!" replied Joe, jumping out of the crane's path and knocking Berridge out of the way before the crane could strike him on the shoulder. "Now what are you going to do with it?"

"Remove whatever's controlling it," Frank yelled, climbing onto the platform at the top of the crane's long arm. "It must be this box with the wires sticking out of it. Got it!"

With a sound of screeching metal, the crane ground to a halt. Frank climbed back off the platform and dropped to the studio floor, a black box with an antenna sticking up from it in his hand.

"This must be what caused it to attack us," he said. "Do you recognize it, Johnny?"

Frank handed the box to Berridge, who examined it for a moment, then shook his head and handed it back.

"No. That's not part of our equipment. Somebody must have hooked that up to the crane controls in the last few hours."

"It must be some sort of remote-control unit, wired directly into the electronics that control the system." said Frank. "It's probably activated by radio waves."

"Then the person who was running that crane could be anywhere in the building—or anywhere in Bayport," said Joe.

"No," said Frank. "He's probably right here in the station. How else could he have known that we were in the studio?"

"Hey!" said Joe, taking the box from Frank and flipping it over. "Look at this!"

He pointed at a metal plate attached to the underside of the box. It read: Another Fine Product from Electronics Attic.

"Electronics Attic!" said Joe. "That's Mediatronics!"

"Could be a coincidence," said Frank. "But I think I'd better take that trip to New York City right now."

"Hurry back," said Joe. "I want to know how the folks at Mediatronics talk their way out of this one!"

Frank arrived at the Bayport train station just in time to catch the one o'clock train for New

York. Two hours later, the train pulled into Manhattan. Frank took a cab from the station to the Mediatronics offices, which were in a tall building with sheer walls of black glass.

Mediatronics occupied the top five floors of the building. Their lobby was spacious and lavishly furnished, full of overstuffed furniture and shag carpeting that looked like it needed regular mowing. The receptionist, a young red-haired woman, sat behind a massive oak desk.

She gave Frank a bored look as he stepped off the elevator. "Can I help you?" she asked. "Do you have an appointment?"

"Er, no," Frank said. "I'd like to talk to Mr. Ettinger, the president of Mediatronics, please."

"I'm afraid I can't help you if you don't have an appointment."

"I wouldn't take more than a few minutes of his time," said Frank. "I'd just like to ask him a few questions, that's all."

"I'm afraid you'll need an appointment," the young woman insisted. "And even if you did have an appointment, it wouldn't do you much good. Mr. Ettinger is out of the office at the moment."

"Oh," said Frank. "Do you know when he'll be back?"

"We're expecting him at any moment. But you really do . . ."

The elevator doors slid open, and a man in a dark suit and gray overcoat stepped into the lobby. He looked to be about fifty years old, with thinning gray hair and dark-framed glasses.

"Oh, Mr. Ettinger," the receptionist said. "This young man was just asking to see you. I told him that he needs an appointment, but—"

"Yes?" said Ettinger. "What was it you wanted to see me about? I'm afraid that my schedule is quite full this afternoon."

"I'm from WBPT-TV in Bayport, Mr. Ettinger. I just wanted to ask you about—"

"WBPT?" snapped Ettinger. His eyebrows creased in anger and his voice took on a threatening tone. "I just finished meeting with your so-called legal representatives. It was one of the least productive meetings of my life! If you people keep refusing to even consider the terms that we offer, I'm not sure that I—"

"Actually, Mr. Ettinger, I wanted to ask you about—"

"If WBPT would like to ask me questions," Ettinger interrupted, "they can send them to me in writing, in care of my lawyers. At the moment, I don't even want to hear the name of your station, do you understand me?"

"Yes," said Frank, "but—"

"No buts! Get out of my building and go tell your bosses that I'm just about fed up with the runaround that they've been giving me. If some progress isn't made in our negotiations by the next meeting, then I'm not responsible for what will happen. Got that?"

68

"I—I think so, but—"

"You're dismissed, young man!" Ettinger snarled. He turned to the receptionist and said: "Julie, see to it that this . . . this person is out of here immediately! If he refuses to leave, you have my permission to call the police!"

"Yes, sir," said the receptionist.

"Mr. Ettinger, I'm investigating some unusual incidents that—" Frank stopped speaking as the president of Mediatronics walked through a pair of heavy wooden doors and loudly slammed them shut.

"I'm afraid you'll have to go now," the receptionist said coldly.

"I got that message," said Frank, walking resignedly back to the elevator.

Scowling, Frank pushed the button for the ground floor. If I could just talk to Ettinger again for a few more seconds, he thought, I could explain the situation, explain that I'm a detective investigating the explosion at the WBPT studios. Of course, Ettinger might still throw him out, but that would only be further evidence that Mediatronics was involved with the Masked Marauder. If Mediatronics was genuinely interested in negotiating fairly for the purchase of WBPT, then they'd also be interested in helping to find the Masked Marauder, not in standing in the way of the investigation.

Only how was he going to get another chance to talk to Ettinger? If Frank entered the lobby again, the receptionist would call the police. He could wait until Ettinger left the office to go home, but that might be hours away, and there was no guarantee that he would get the chance even then. No. He had to get back into the Mediatronics office somehow.

The elevator opened and Frank walked out into the main lobby of the building. People hurried past, briefcases and shopping bags in hand, oblivious to his presence. In one corner of the lobby, a painter in a spattered uniform was sitting on a stool, sipping coffee from a cardboard cup. Frank strolled casually to where the painter was sitting.

"Excuse me," Frank said. "Are you the painter we called to do the touch-up work for the Easy-Goes-It Travel Agency?"

"Huh?" said the painter. "Never heard of it. I was just refinishing the lobby here, but this is my coffee break."

Frank pointed to a painter's smock lying on the floor next to one of the stools.

"Who does that belong to?" he asked.

"Oh, that's Lenny's," the painter explained. "Lenny got sick from all the paint fumes and had to go home for the afternoon. Lenny's got some kind of allergy to paint fumes. I never could figure how he got into this business to begin with."

"Never mind," said Frank. "I don't suppose Lenny would mind if I borrowed his smock and his paint can and maybe a brush?"

"I'm not too sure," the painter said hesitantly. "Lenny might be mad if I let just anybody walk off with his stuff."

"No problem," said Frank. "If Lenny has any questions, just tell him to call the Easy-Goes-It Travel Agency and talk to Frank. I'm sure I can explain the situation to his satisfaction. You see, we called for a painter and he hasn't shown up yet and, well, we have some important clients coming in this afternoon . . ."

"Okay, okay," said the painter. "I can't see it would make much difference, anyway, what with Lenny out sick and all. What did you say you needed? The smock and some paint and a brush—"

"And, uh, maybe that cap that you're wearing," said Frank.

Ten minutes later, Frank walked back out of the elevator and into the offices of Mediatronics, Inc. He wore the painter's cap pulled low over his face and stared down at the carpet as he walked in front of the receptionist, hoping that she wouldn't recognize him. He was carrying the bucket of paint in one hand and the brush in the other, the painter's smock covering the clothes that the receptionist had seen him in earlier.

"Emergency paint job," he mumbled, walking quickly toward the double doors through which he had seen Ettinger vanish.

71

"Excuse me?" asked the receptionist. "I don't remember calling for a painter."

"Well, somebody did," Frank muttered.

"I'll have to check," she said. "Wait here while I talk to the office manager."

"Sorry, lady," Frank said, trying to make his voice sound deeper. "Union rules. I get off work at four-thirty, and if I ain't finished by then I gotta leave WET PAINT signs on all your doors and drop cloths on your furniture . . ."

"What?" asked the confused receptionist.

"This'll just take a minute," mumbled Frank. "The person who called said that Mr. Ettinger was gonna fire everybody in sight if they didn't get the frammis painted before the meeting with whosis . . ."

"Well, I'm not sure . . ."

"Be done in a flash," Frank announced, darting for the wooden doors. He had opened them and gotten halfway through before the receptionist could gather her wits.

"You really shouldn't—" she was saying as Frank slammed the doors closed.

Whew! thought Frank, pulling the cap back from his forehead. I'd better move fast before the receptionist thinks to call Mr. Ettinger and verify my story. Now where do you suppose this guy has his office?

Frank was standing in a carpeted hallway with doors branching off to both sides. Each door had a name printed on it, but none of them was

Ettinger's. He walked rapidly to the far end of the hall, where it made an L-shaped turn to the left. At the end of the second section of hallway was a pair of double doors with a name painted on them in bright blue letters. Warren Ettinger, President, it read.

Ettinger's office! thought Frank gleefully.

Frank was practically running toward the office when a woman stepped out of a door and into the hallway in front of him. She had carefully combed gray hair and a pair of tortoise-shell glasses that she seemed to peer over with an imperious expression.

"Yes?" she said. "Can I help you? I don't recall requesting a painter."

"The office manager called us," said Frank nervously, remembering what the receptionist had said a moment earlier. He stood uneasily as the woman stared at him. He had been prepared to talk his way past the receptionist, but he wasn't thrilled at having to bluff his way into the Mediatronics offices a second time.

"I *am* the office manager," the woman declared haughtily, "and I did not call for you!"

"Ah, er," stammered Frank desperately, "well, I *thought* it was the office manager. Maybe it was somebody else. You know how these things get confused."

"Yes," the woman replied dubiously. "We'll see about that. Follow me to my office, young man, and we'll see if we can get this straightened

73

out. I don't like it when things go on in this office that I don't know about!"

The woman brushed past Frank and walked away from Ettinger's office. Then she paused and turned back, waiting for Frank to follow. With a shrug of resignation, Frank walked after her.

As soon as she had gone around the corner, however, Frank spun on his heels and raced back toward Ettinger's office, thankful that he had thought to wear running shoes. If he could just have a few seconds to talk to Ettinger, he was sure that he could get things worked out.

At Ettinger's door, he raised his hand to knock, then paused. Ettinger's voice boomed out loudly from inside. It sounded as though he were talking on the telephone.

"I don't care what those idiots at that two-bit TV station think!" he declared loudly. "Tell them that this is their last chance!"

Is he talking about WBPT? Frank wondered. It sure sounded like it.

"If they don't drop their price by tomorrow," Ettinger continued in an angry voice, "tell them it will be too late.

"There won't be any TV station left to sell!"

8 Tomorrow Is Doomsday

While Frank Hardy was in New York, his brother, Joe, was back in Bayport, laying a trap for the Masked Marauder. A police detective named Bryce Thomas explained what was going to happen.

"This Marauder guy expects to find a briefcase full of bills at the corner of Chelmsley Avenue and Fisherman's Lane," said Thomas. "He wants somebody to be standing there with the briefcase and he doesn't want it to be a cop."

Joe, seated across from Thomas in Mona's office, nodded. "That's where I come in, right?"

"Right," said Thomas. "You'll be holding the briefcase. When somebody asks for it, you give it to him."

"Just like that?"

"Just like that," agreed Thomas. "We'll be watching the whole thing. Whoever takes the briefcase won't get very far."

"There won't be any money in the briefcase, will there?" asked Joe.

"No," said Thomas. "We're stuffing it full of old newspapers, so that it'll have the right weight."

"What if the Marauder notices that I'm not alone?" asked Joe.

"He won't. We'll have our best undercover people on the job. The Marauder will never know he's being watched."

"Sounds good," said Joe. "When should I be there?"

"The Marauder wants to pick up the briefcase at nine o'clock this evening. You'll be there at five minutes of. Don't be late."

"You can bet I won't," said Joe. Then, as he and Thomas stood to leave the office: "I just wish Frank could be here for this."

At five minutes of nine that evening, Joe was standing at the corner of Chelmsley Avenue and Fisherman's Lane, a large, dark briefcase in his hand, waiting for the Marauder. It wasn't the best neighborhood in Bayport. In fact, it could reasonably be called a slum. Joe was feeling nervous just standing there, minding his own business.

The sun had gone down about fifteen minutes earlier and the sky was still grayish blue. People wandered about aimlessly. Cars honked their horns as they passed. Loud music played out of windows and from boom boxes carried by passing teenagers.

So where's the Marauder? Joe wondered, cautiously scanning the crowds of people around him. How am I even going to know him when I see him?

For that matter, where were the police? He looked around and saw no sign of the undercover officers that Bryce Thomas had assured him would be watching. Well, he thought, that makes sense. If I could spot them that easily, they wouldn't be very good undercover police, would they?

Not far from where Joe stood, a crowd of restless-looking teenagers was hanging around in front of an all-night pool hall, laughing and making rowdy noises. Joe didn't recognize any of them. Every few minutes, one of them looked curiously in Joe's direction, as though he was trying to figure out what Joe was doing there. Joe ignored him, or at least tried to.

Joe glanced at his watch. One minute of nine. Will the Marauder get here on time, he wondered, or will I end up standing here all night, waiting?

"Hey, you!" said a voice just over his shoulder.

Joe turned to see one of the teenagers who had been hanging around in front of the pool hall, standing only a few feet away.

"That's right, boy," the teenager said with a smirk. "You!"

"Yeah?" said Joe. "What do you want?"

"Nothing. We were just wondering what you were doing here, that's all. You don't look like nobody I've ever seen in this part of town before."

"I'm not from around here," said Joe.

"I bet," the teenager said. "Maybe we don't like folks like you hangin' around here, either."

Joe ignored him, resisting the urge to tell him to get lost. The other teenagers from the pool hall were watching their conversation with interest, and Joe didn't want to start trouble, especially with the Marauder due to show up at any second.

Suddenly the teenager lunged at Joe, knocked him backward against a wall, snatched the briefcase from Joe's hands, and darted into the street.

"So long, sucker!" he shouted at Joe.

"Hey!" Joe yelled in surprise. "Come back with that!"

He was cut off by the sharp screech of a police siren. A bright flashing light appeared on the dashboard of a nearby car and Joe suddenly realized that the men inside the car were the undercover police officers who had been watching him. Two of them leaped out of the car and ran after the teenager who had snatched the briefcase. Then the driver pulled the car into the street and joined the chase.

The briefcase snatcher threw a startled glance over his shoulder and began running twice as fast for the opposite side of the street. Joe, recovering

78

from his surprise, began running after the thief, too. He reached the other side of the street just in time to see the teenager duck into a narrow alley.

Bryce Thomas appeared out of nowhere and shouted instructions to the two undercover police officers.

"You!" he yelled at one of them. "Go around that way and head him off on the other side of the block. We'll go this way!"

He ran into the alley and waved for Joe to follow him. The teenager with the briefcase was about halfway to the other end of the alley and running fast. Joe and Thomas sprinted after him at full speed.

"Think he's the Marauder?" gasped Thomas as he ran.

"I don't know," said Joe. "I thought he just wanted to give me a hard time until he grabbed the briefcase."

At the other end of the alley, the teenager ran directly in front of a car, which squealed to a halt inches before it ran him down. Ignoring the shouts of the angry driver, the teenager leaped across the car's hood and landed running on the other side.

Joe and Thomas darted out of the alley about ten feet behind him. The teenager put on a burst of speed, then saw one of the plainclothes officers round the corner ahead of him. The plain-clothes officer dropped to one knee and pulled a gun.

The teenager dropped the briefcase and stopped running.

"What is this?" he shouted. "What are you guys after me for? I didn't do nothin' wrong!"

"You always run like that when you 'didn't do nothin' wrong?'" asked Thomas, coming up behind him.

"I always run when I see a bunch of big dudes comin' after me," explained the teenager. "I thought you were gonna mug me or somethin'."

"Sure you did," said Thomas. "Where'd you get that briefcase?"

"What briefcase? You mean the one on the ground there? Never seen it before."

"We've got five witnesses that saw you snatch it off Joe here," Thomas said patiently. "Why'd you take it?"

"I don't have to tell you nothin'," the teenager said belligerently.

"Then you can tell us down at the station house. Have it your way."

"All right, all right," the teenager said. "This guy told me that there'd be somebody at the corner tonight with a briefcase. He gave me ten bucks to snatch it for him. He said he'd give me another ten bucks when I gave it to him."

"What did the guy look like?" asked Thomas.

"I don't know," the teenager said.

"You don't know?" replied Thomas dubiously. "What do you mean, you don't know? Was he wearing a mask or something?"

"Yeah," said the teenager. "How did you know? He was wearin' a mask like wrestlers wear. Black and kind of leathery."

Joe and Bryce Thomas exchanged startled glances. *The Marauder!*

"Where were you supposed to meet him?" Thomas asked.

"Grommet Park," the teenager said. "Next to the fountain. I was on my way there now."

Thomas rubbed his head. "All right," he said. "Get out of here. And don't pull anything like this again, you hear? You make any more trouble, I'll have you in jail before you can count to three."

Grommet Park was three blocks north of where they had apprehended the teenager. It was a small park, only one city block in size, but it was thick with trees and shrubbery, surrounding a large fountain. Joe and the party of police officers made their way carefully into the center of the park, on the alert for any sign of movement.

There was nobody there. The fountain burbled quietly. A soft wind sighed through the trees and bushes.

"No sign of the Marauder," said Thomas.

"Now what?" said Joe. "Do you suppose he'll show up?"

"I doubt it," said Thomas. "Not after seeing us here."

"Look at this," shouted one of the plainclothes officers.

Perched on the edge of the fountain was a white paper envelope. Thomas took the envelope and examined it. Nothing was written on it.

He ripped it open. After staring at it for a minute, he handed it to Joe.

"It's not good news," he said. "Looks like we went to all this trouble for nothing."

Joe read the note. It was neatly typed, on a sheet of white paper. It said:

I told you not to bring any cops!
Now you've really blown it!
Tomorrow is Doomsday for WBPT!
—The Masked Marauder

9 Explosive Interview

"That bit about there not being 'any TV station left to sell' sounds like a pretty clear threat to me!" said Joe, slathering jelly onto a piece of fresh toast. It was the morning after Frank's trip to New York and Joe's adventure with the police. Joe and Frank were seated at their dining room table, devouring breakfast, while their aunt Gertrude bustled happily in and out of the kitchen.

"Agreed," said Frank. "I wish I'd had the chance to hear more, but the office manager grabbed me by the neck before I could confront Ettinger. She and the receptionist practically *threw* me into the elevator. I'm lucky they didn't have me arrested. So how did things go with you?"

"Not so hot," Joe reported. "We tried to pass a briefcase stuffed with newspapers to the Marauder last night, but the plan backfired." Joe told Frank what had happened. "Now the Marauder's ticked off at us and he's going to go ahead with his plans to do whatever it is he's planning to do."

"Rough break," said Frank. "Well, it's not like we weren't expecting it, anyway."

"There's just one thing that bothers me," said Joe. "At the end of the chase, we found a typed note from the Marauder, telling us that we'd blown it."

"So?"

"So when did the Marauder have time to *type* a note? He must have put it on the fountain right before we got there."

"Maybe he does this a lot," suggested Frank. "He may keep form letters."

"Why do I doubt that?" asked Joe.

Frank shrugged. "So how did things go at the TV station after I left?"

"Pretty good," said Joe. "We've got everything set up for our Crimestoppers, Inc., spot this afternoon. Johnny and I wrote a script for it. You might want to read it before we go on."

"I'm impressed!" Frank laughed. "Not only are you a TV star and a national hero, but now you're a writer, too. Will wonders never cease?"

"I'm just a man of many talents," Joe said modestly. "I also suggested to Johnny that he leave one of the cameras running in Studio A tonight and this morning, so that if the Marauder shows up again we can get a picture of him on tape. Our *own* tape!"

"Good idea. But what if he doesn't hit Studio A this time?"

"We can't cover the whole place with cameras," replied Joe reasonably. "But I figure we might get lucky. Oh . . . I discovered something else interesting. Remember that VCR cassette that the Marauder spliced into the transmitter yesterday? Guess what the brand name on it is?"

"Electronics Attic?" suggested Frank.

"You got it," said Joe.

"Maybe the Marauder's a big fan of their stores."

"You still believe that after what Ettinger said yesterday?"

"I don't know what to believe," said Frank. "I *do* know that I'm going to tell Mona and Amberson to be very careful around Ettinger and his bunch."

"I'll second that," said Joe.

"Whatever are you boys talking about?" asked Aunt Gertrude, appearing from the kitchen with a large plate of muffins in her hand. "I heard about that explosion at the TV station on Monday. I'm not sure it's safe for you boys to be there. And what's this about you being on television again today?"

"Haven't you heard, Aunt Gertrude?" said Frank with a straight face. "Joe's going to be a

85

television star. I expect he'll be living in Beverly Hills before the month is out, riding in a chauffeured limousine, signing autographs, giving interviews to magazines."

"Joe Hardy!" said Aunt Gertrude indignantly. "You know you haven't even finished school yet! Of course, it does sound a lot safer than this detective work that you boys keep getting caught up in—"

"Oops, sorry, Aunt Gertrude!" Joe interrupted. "Gotta go! They're expecting us at the station now. Can't be late!"

"Aren't you even going to take some of my muffins?"

"No time, Aunt Gertrude," said Joe. "Well, er, maybe two . . ."

"Make that four," added Frank.

At the station, Frank and Joe found Mona and Amberson having a conference in the station manager's office. The brothers told them about Frank's experience in New York. Mona looked worried by the news, but Amberson was strangely unconcerned.

"Forget about Mediatronics," Amberson said. "Just keep your eyes open here at the station. That's what you were hired for."

"What do you mean, forget about Mediatronics?" shouted Joe. "After this Ettinger guy said there wouldn't be 'any TV station left to sell'? That sounds like a pretty serious threat to me!"

"I'll worry about that," said Amberson mysteriously. "By the way, I hear that your idea for catching the Marauder last night didn't work."

Joe shrugged. "He was too smart for us, I guess. He sent some kid in to snatch the briefcase. The police went for the kid and the Marauder bugged out. I guess they showed you the note that he left."

"Yeah," growled Amberson. "It really made my day."

"At least," said Frank, "the police will be guarding the station today. Maybe the Marauder won't be able to get in."

Amberson puffed on his cigar for a moment, then gave the brothers a sour look. "I wonder why that doesn't make me feel any better." he said.

By midafternoon, the set for that day's "Faces and Places" had already been erected in Studio A. Joe showed Frank the props that he'd picked out for their demonstration: a couple of doors in stand-alone frames with locks attached. Frank glanced over the script, attempting to memorize his lines.

"You're not going to come down with another case of stage fright, are you?" Frank asked Joe.

His brother gave him an indignant look. "We

big-time TV stars don't *get* stage fright," he said. "I'm an old pro now. A national hero, too. Don't forget that."

The police were in evidence around the studio. Frank noticed a stocky officer standing watch next to the rear door of the studio and another in the hallway just outside the main door.

A half hour before the show started, the audience began to file in. This time, the studio seats were filled right up to the aisles with what appeared to be members of the Wayne Clintock Fan Club, waiting noisily for their hero to arrive.

"I wonder if they'll be so anxious to see old Wayne after they get a look at 'Mrs. Brody's Boardinghouse'?" asked Joe.

"Sure they will," said Frank. "If they can stop laughing long enough."

Mona stopped by briefly to check whether the Hardys were prepared for their Crimestoppers spot. She looked nervous and distracted.

"I just hope Bill Amberson knows what he's doing," she said. "If anybody gets hurt, I'll never forgive myself for not insisting that we close the station down. Have you seen anything suspicious going on?"

"No," said Frank. "Not yet. And the police are here in case there's trouble."

"That's something, at least," said Mona. "Well, if you need me, I'll be watching from the director's booth.

"Oh," she added, "I do have some good news.

Wayne Clintock has agreed to let us run 'Mrs. Brody's Boardinghouse.' Johnny tells me that he told you yesterday about our negotiations with Clintock, right?"

The brothers nodded.

"We finally reached a satisfactory agreement with him yesterday," she continued. "Clintock will be making the announcement on the air today," Mona continued. "Apparently Clintock believes that if you can't beat 'em, you join 'em. He'll even be doing a publicity tour for us. For a substantial fee, of course."

Five minutes before airtime, Matt Freeman appeared and took his seat on the set. He chatted with the audience for a moment, telling a few jokes, drawing cheers every time the name Wayne Clintock was mentioned.

When Clintock himself walked out, the audience went crazy. They chanted his name and stomped their feet. One of the police officers guarding the door had to stand in the aisle briefly to keep the audience from storming the stage.

"Wayne! Wayne!" the audience shouted.

Clintock milked the response for all it was worth. He swaggered a little as he walked to his seat, saluted his fans, and smiled at them shyly. The audience cheered even louder.

When the red light appeared on one of the cameras, Freeman raised his hands to silence the studio audience, then addressed the viewers at home.

"We have a special treat for 'Faces and Places' viewers today," he announced. "We'll be talking with one of the best-loved actors in America, a man who needs no introduction to his millions of loyal fans, many of whom are in our studio audience and many more of whom, I'm sure, are in our home audience. Of course I'm talking about the star of the brand-new motion picture *Badge of Honor* . . . Wayne Clintock!"

The audience leaped to its feet and began cheering again. Freeman had to motion them to silence so that he could finish his introduction. "Wayne will be making an important announcement this afternoon, one that I'm sure all WBPT viewers will find extremely exciting. In addition, we'll have a second appearance by those ever-popular Bayport detectives, Frank and Joe Hardy, who will be inaugurating a new feature on 'Faces and Places' that we call 'Crimestoppers, Inc.' So I'm sure you'll want to stay tuned for that."

Freeman turned to his guest. "I'd like to thank you for being with us today, Wayne," he said.

"It's my pleasure, Matt," drawled Clintock.

"So tell us about your new movie, Wayne . . ."

Joe looked at Frank and whispered, "So that's what it's like to be a star, huh? Just go on TV shows, wave to your fans, and act charming? I think I can handle it."

"You might be expected to work occasionally, too," suggested Frank.

"Hey, how much work can it be? Memorize a

90

few lines, stand in front of a camera and look tough, shoot toy guns. It sure sounds like the life for me!"

"So, Wayne," Matt Freeman was saying, "I'm told that WBPT viewers will be getting a look at a Wayne Clintock they've never seen before."

"Er, that's right, Matt," Clintock said uneasily. "Not many people know this, but I starred in a television series back in the early 1950s, right after I got out of high school."

"And we'll be showing that series right here on WBPT in the weeks to come," said Freeman.

"So I'm told," said Clintock. "I had, uh, thought that any copies of the series had disappeared years ago. We worked live in those days, of course."

"But," Freeman interjected, "we made a historical discovery here at WBPT just a few weeks ago. Fifty episodes of a classic TV series called 'Mrs. Brody's Boardinghouse' were discovered in our archives. And, in fact, we have them right here."

An engineer appeared from one side of the room, dragging a large wooden flat covered with a dark tarpaulin. He placed the flat next to the set, just within range of the camera. Then he pulled off the tarpaulin, revealing a large pile of old film canisters.

"There they are, ladies and gentlemen! All fifty episodes of the series, each one of them featuring your favorite star and mine, Wayne Clintock!"

91

The fans in the audience started cheering again, and Clintock smiled at them a little nervously.

"I wonder what he's thinking?" asked Frank.

"Probably hoping the ground will open and swallow the whole stack of kinescopes," said Joe. "Hey, do you smell something funny?"

"No, I . . ." Frank sniffed the air experimentally. "Yeah, I do. It smells like—"

"Look over there!" said Joe. "Something's dripping from the ceiling!"

Frank looked up. Sure enough, a thin stream of liquid was pouring down from the studio ceiling and puddling on the floor. The puddle was already beginning to overflow in the direction of the set.

"Gasoline!" said Frank. "It smells like gasoline!"

"We've got to stop the show!" shouted Joe. "It's the Marauder! He must have—"

Before Joe could finish his sentence, there was a sharp explosion from overhead. A column of flame came rushing down from the ceiling, traveling along the stream of gasoline. Then it struck the puddle that had formed underneath the stream.

The floor of the studio burst into bright orange flames!

10 Panic!

For two or three seconds the studio was in absolute silence, except for the crackling of flames. Then Wayne Clintock and Matt Freeman threw themselves out of their chairs as the flames shot onto the set. The audience began to scream.

"Calm down!" Joe yelled. "The fire sprinklers should go on any second." But the blaze spread, and there was no sign of the system kicking in. Joe glanced around nervously. "Let's get out of here."

"Which way?" asked Frank. "We can't get to the back door! The fire is in the way!"

"And the front doors are blocked by the studio audience. Look at those people! They're falling all over themselves! Didn't anybody ever tell them to stay calm in case of an emergency?"

The Wayne Clintock Fan Club had turned into a hysterical mass of humanity, clawing its way toward the door in blind panic. The police were trying to keep order and Clintock himself was shouting at them to keep calm, but his voice was lost in the general tumult.

Suddenly, as if by magic, Bill Amberson came bursting out of the crowd, running toward the set.

"The kinescopes!" he shouted. "The kinescopes are on fire!"

Mona appeared just behind him. She waved at the Hardy brothers, a frantic look on her face.

"Stop him!" she shouted. "He thinks he can save the films!"

"Hey!" said Joe, grabbing Amberson by one arm as Frank grabbed the other. "You can't go near those things! You want to turn yourself into a french fry?" He waved a hand toward the stack of film canisters, which was already enveloped by the raging inferno.

"I've *got* to get them!" he shouted, struggling to break loose. "They're our only chance to keep the station from going bankrupt! I can't let them burn! Now we'll be *forced* to sell to Mediatronics!"

"It's too late!" said Frank, dragging Amberson toward the door. The fire was already so intense that he could feel it sizzling against his exposed flesh. "The kinescopes are already burning! There's nothing you can do now!"

Even as Frank spoke, the film canisters began to explode, one after another, from the pressure of the burning celluloid inside. Hot fragments of metal and plastic shot into the air. Realizing that there was no chance of saving the films, Amberson stopped struggling as Frank and Joe urged him toward the door.

The fire had almost spread to the seats where the audience had been moments before. Miraculously, the last of Clintock's hysterical fans squeezed through the door just in time to let Frank, Joe, and Amberson escape into the hallway. A dark cloud of smoke billowed out behind them. Sirens screeched loudly from the parking lot, and the first battalion of firefighters was already racing down the hallway to the studio.

A fire lieutenant stood shaking his head. "We've discovered signs of sabotage in the sprinkler system—that's given the fire a real head start." He headed down the hall. "We'll do our best to keep it from doing any more damage."

"It's already done enough damage!" Amberson moaned. "Gone! All gone! All fifty kinescopes, up in smoke! We were going to make a fortune off those things! We might as well let the whole place burn down now!"

"Don't say that, Mr. Amberson," said Mona, coming up behind them in the hallway. "As long as we still own the studio, there's a chance that we can raise the money to keep it alive."

"How?" Amberson said, slumping against a wall. "You can't just hold a bake sale to save a television station. We'll have to sell out to Mediatronics. We have no choice." Amberson's

95

eyes went blank and he seemed to stare numbly into space. He slumped toward the floor, as though there were a heavy weight pressing on his shoulders.

"Help me get him outside," Mona said to the Hardys. "Into the parking lot, where he'll be safe."

Frank and Joe lifted the unprotesting Amberson by the arms and led him to the parking lot, where the audience and crew from "Faces and Places" had already gathered. Bright red fire trucks sat between the rows of cars, and more were arriving by the minute. Greasy black smoke curled upward into the sky above the station.

Frank pulled Joe off to one side. "So what do you think?" he asked, when they were out of earshot of the others. "About the fire, I mean?"

"Same thing you do, I'll bet. I think that whoever caused this fire—our friend the Masked Marauder, whoever he is—didn't care about the money in that briefcase last night. He probably never expected Amberson to fork over a penny. That's why he typed that note in advance. I think what he was really after were those kinescopes."

"Brilliant deduction," said Frank. "I might make a detective out of you yet. So who stands to profit from destroying the kinescopes?"

"Mediatronics, for one," said Joe. "We just heard Amberson say that the fire will force him to sell out. Mediatronics will get their TV studio and their fourth network."

". . . which makes them Suspect Number One," said Frank. "Now who else would want those films out of the way?"

"Wayne Clintock?" suggested Joe.

"Uh-huh. Like Johnny Berridge said, Clintock would probably prefer that those kinescopes had stayed lost for another hundred years or so. Well, it looks like he got his wish. Which makes him Suspect Number Two."

"I just wish we had some hard evidence against either one of them," said Joe.

"Maybe we do—the videotape from the camera Johnny left running in the studio last night."

Joe snapped his fingers. "Right! I'd forgotten about that! I hope the tape didn't go up in smoke along with the kinescopes."

"Why don't we ask Johnny?" Frank suggested. "He's standing right there."

The young cameraman was staring at the smoke pouring from the WBPT building, a distraught look on his face. "Oh, hello, Frank, Joe," he said vaguely as they came up beside him. "This is terrible, isn't it? That might be my job burning up in there."

"It's pretty terrible," agreed Joe. "Uh, listen, did you make that videotape I asked you to make last night? The one in Studio A?"

"Videotape?" repeated Berridge. "Oh, yeah, I . . ." He suddenly snapped to attention, his worries forgotten. "That's right! We may have pictures of the Marauder himself! I've got two

97

full tape cartridges! I left them in my office, on top of my desk!"

"Can we look at them?" asked Frank. "That's an awful lot of tape, but if the Marauder is in there someplace . . ."

"Sure," said Berridge. "We can use the mobile van. There's a tape deck in there. We'll just do a forward scan through the tape until something happens. Shouldn't take too long."

"The mobile van?" asked Joe. "What's that?"

Berridge pointed to a nearby panel truck with the letters *WBPT* written on its side in bright colors. "It's our portable videotape studio. We use it for news programs, on-the-spot reports, that kind of thing. Hang on while I get the tapes!"

Berridge ran back to the building. When he reached it, the fire chief stopped him from entering. They spoke for a moment, then Berridge went into the building through a side door. Not far away, firefighters were still squirting long columns of water at the west wall of Studio A. The smoke had stopped pouring out now. The fire was under control.

Minutes later, Berridge reappeared, a stricken look on his face. He was empty-handed.

"Where are the tapes?" Joe asked.

"I . . . I don't know," Berridge replied. "They were in my office, on the desk. They're not there now! I don't know what happened to them!"

"Oh, that's just great!" said Joe. "We've probably got a picture of the Masked Marauder without his mask and now we can't find it. Terrific!"

"A picture of the Masked Marauder?" asked Mona, who had come up to see what was going on. "What kind of picture?"

"Johnny left a camera running in Studio A last night and this morning. We may have a picture of the Marauder planting the bomb."

"Why, that's great!" said Mona. "Why don't we—"

"Look at the tapes?" finished Joe. "Because they've vanished, that's why."

"I'm sorry, guys," said Berridge. "I should have taken better care of them. I guess I couldn't bring myself to believe in the Marauder's dooms-day threat. I really didn't think he'd set off another bomb. And he didn't take any chances on failing, either. The fire chief told me someone had cut off the water to the sprinkler system."

"That figures," said Joe. "He probably stole the tapes, too. But don't feel bad, Johnny. You didn't have any reason to think that somebody might snatch them, after all."

"How did the Marauder even know what was on the tapes?" asked Frank.

"I don't know," said Johnny. "Maybe this guy has X-ray eyes. Or practices telepathy."

"That's just what we need." Frank laughed. "An evil superman!"

"So what do we do now?" asked Joe.

"Same thing we were doing before," said Frank. "Keep our eyes open."

"What good will that do now?" asked Joe. "The Marauder's already struck, and he probably won't strike again."

"Maybe the tapes will turn up," Frank said hopefully.

"I'll tell you what you can be doing," said Mona. "Preparing for your Crimestoppers spot on tomorrow's show."

"Huh?" said the brothers in chorus.

"You're kidding!" said Joe.

"You mean you're still going to be producing 'Faces and Places'—even after the fire in the studio? It'll take weeks to clean up the mess in there!"

"The show must go on," said Mona. "Fortunately, the fire was confined to Studio A. We have a smaller studio that we can use while Studio A is being repaired."

"Let me guess," said Joe. "It's called Studio B."

"Now you're catching on," said Mona. "It's a little cramped compared to Studio A, but it's adequate."

"I guess we can do the same spot that we didn't have a chance to do today," said Frank.

"Actually," said Mona, "I'd prefer it if you'd work up some kind of remote presentation."

"Remote?" asked Joe.

"From outside the studio," said Mona. "Like I

100

said, Studio B is a little cramped and I'm not sure we have room for the two of you on the set along with Matt. But you and Johnny can use the mobile van to broadcast from somewhere outside the studio. Anywhere in Bayport, in fact."

"How about the Waterview Apartments?" said Frank. "That was where the High Rise Bandit was operating a couple of months ago."

"Yeah," said Joe. "We can show viewers how he broke into apartments and what they can do to prevent some other burglar from breaking into theirs in the same way."

"Good idea, boys," said Mona. "I knew you two would fit right into 'Faces and Places' when I hired you. I'll call ahead and arrange things with the Waterview management."

"What about Amberson?" Frank asked. "Is he okay?"

"I think so," said Mona. "He's a little stunned, but I think he's coming around. It's not every day that he sees his livelihood go up in flames. I'm still a little numb myself."

"I guess we all are," said Joe. "But, boy, I wish we had those tapes. Now the Marauder may get away scot-free!"

"It's not too late," Mona said. "The police are looking for him. Maybe they'll find some clues in the studio."

"Yeah," said Joe without enthusiasm. "Maybe."

"Listen," said Mona. "Why don't you boys take

101

the rest of the afternoon off? You and Johnny can prepare the Crimestoppers spot in the morning. There's no rush."

"Sure," said Berridge. "I'll have the remote van ready for you tomorrow morning."

"I guess we can use the break," said Frank. "This has been a tough day."

"Then I'll see you in the morning," said Mona. "Get a good night's rest."

"So where did we leave the Hardy van?" asked Joe. "It seems like about a hundred years since we arrived at the station this morning."

"I know what you mean," said Frank. "The van's over this way. Come on."

"What's that crowd doing in front of the station?" asked Joe. "Over there." He gestured toward a cluster of people milling around opposite the front doors.

"Probably rubberneckers, gawking at the fire. Maybe they just like to watch fire trucks."

"No," said Joe. "Look at the sign that guy's carrying. It must be the rest of the Wayne Clintock Fan Club."

"Yeah, the ones who weren't lucky enough to get into the studio for the show."

"Real lucky. The ones who did get in almost got burned up for the privilege. Listen to those guys. . . ."

A singsong chant was coming from the crowd. They were shouting, "We want Wayne! We want Wayne!" over and over again.

"Let's avoid that bunch," said Frank. "I like Wayne Clintock's movies, too, but those people look a little weird."

"Fine with me," said Joe. Then, "Uh-oh. Look at that guy over there, skulking through the bushes. He doesn't look like he belongs to the fan club."

"Where?" asked Frank, scanning the side of the building until he spotted the suspicious-looking figure that Joe was referring to. "Oh, yeah. And he's wearing a green Army fatigue jacket. Isn't that what Johnny Berridge said the guy who attacked him in the equipment room was wearing?"

"Right!" cried Joe. "That must be the Masked Marauder!"

11 Return to the Scene

"Get him!" shouted Joe. "This may be our last chance!"

The two of them sprinted toward the building. The figure in the fatigue jacket apparently heard them coming, because he suddenly started running away from them, toward the members of the Wayne Clintock Fan Club.

"He's heading into the crowd!" cried Frank. "I think we've got him! Come on!"

The green-jacketed figure vanished among the milling fans, with Frank and Joe hot on his trail. But as the Hardys rushed through the chanting fans in pursuit of the Marauder, a voice suddenly cried out: "Hey! I recognize that guy!"

Joe turned and saw a man in a suede jacket and cowboy boots, carrying a sign that read: Wayne Clintock's Number-One Fan. He was startled to realize that the man was pointing at him. "Huh?"

Joe said, trying to push another fan-club member out of his path.

"That's Joe Hardy!" the sign-carrying man cried. "The guy who was on television Monday. The one who was on all the newscasts!"

"Hey, yeah!" shouted a girl in a spangled cheerleader's outfit. "He's the one who saved that guy's life! I want his autograph!"

Someone thrust a pen and a piece of paper in Joe's face. "Would you sign this?" asked a whining voice. "I'll let you sign the same page that Wayne Clintock is going to sign!"

"Are you crazy?" shouted Joe. "I just want to get through here."

"Yeah, let us through," screamed Frank. "This is an emergency! Let us through!"

A plump hand grabbed Frank's shoulder. "Are you anybody famous?" asked a teenage boy.

"No!" snapped Frank. "And neither is my brother! Get out of our way!"

"That's Joe Hardy's brother!" a young girl shouted. "I want to get his autograph, too!"

Somebody thrust an autograph book into Joe's hand. He tossed it angrily to the ground and shouted, "We've lost him, Frank! I don't see any sign of the Marauder!"

"Maybe he went into the building," Frank said. "Come on! Let's go back inside."

"You guys aren't very nice," someone snarled. "Maybe we don't want your autographs after all!"

"Yeah!" agreed a chorus of voices. "Who needs you guys anyway? We want Wayne!"

The crowd finally parted and let Frank and Joe through. Together, they stumbled up to the front door of the building, past a police guard who recognized them and let them through. When quizzed by the Hardys, the guard confessed that he wasn't sure whether a person in a green fatigue jacket had entered there or not; he hadn't been paying close attention.

"Okay," said Joe. "Assuming the Marauder *did* come through here, where do you think he went next?"

"Maybe he headed back to the studio," Frank said. "He could have forgotten some crucial piece of evidence."

"And he went back to get it!" Joe said. "Okay, let's check out Studio A."

The air inside the station was thick with smoke. Firefighters were walking back and forth in puddles of water. There were police officers standing guard outside the door to Studio A. When Frank and Joe tried to get inside, they were politely turned away.

"The studio's in pretty bad shape, boys," one officer said. "We've got orders not to let anybody in."

"Have you seen a guy in a green fatigue jacket come this way?" Frank asked.

"I don't think so," the officer told them. "Sorry."

"So what next?" Frank asked Joe.

"I'm not sure," Joe said, leading Frank down a nearby hallway. "I'd still like to get a look in that studio. The Marauder might sneak in the back way."

"If *he* can sneak in," suggested Frank, "so can we. Where's the back door?"

"I've got a better idea," said Joe. "When I was up on that catwalk on Monday, I noticed a door leading into the upper levels of the studio."

"Directly onto the catwalks?" Frank asked.

"Yeah. From up there, we'd have a view of the whole studio, so if the Marauder is in there, we can't miss him."

"Perfect!" said Frank. "I'm sure nobody would mind if we just took a look at the studio from the catwalks."

"Come on," said Joe. "The stairs are over here."

Together, the Hardys bounded up a flight of stairs. In the hallway on the next floor was a sign that said Studio A Lighting Area with an arrow pointing to the right.

"That must be it," said Frank.

About fifty feet farther along the hallway was a doorway labeled Studio A Catwalks. Before the Hardys could reach the door, however, they saw a furtive figure slip inside.

"Who was that?" asked Frank.

"I don't know," replied Joe. "I didn't get a

look at his face. He wasn't wearing a green jacket, though."

"Maybe he slipped it off after we recognized him. Maybe it also occurred to the Marauder that he could get into the studio through the catwalks."

"Let's check this out," said Joe, tiptoeing to the door. "Come on."

Joe quietly opened the door to the catwalks. A thick odor of smoke poured out and into the Hardys' nostrils.

"Whew!" said Frank. "I hope we can breathe in there!"

"I plan to hold my breath," whispered Joe. "We should have brought along gas masks."

Just inside the door was a metal platform with a guardrail running alongside it. Joe walked stealthily onto the platform, crouching so that the guardrail would at least partially shield him from the view of anyone watching the door. Frank followed, easing the door closed behind him. No lights were on in this upper part of the studio. But from below, emergency lights cast a dim glow, filling the catwalks with eerie shadows.

Beyond the guardrail, the Hardys had a good view of Studio A—or what was left of Studio A. The "Faces and Places" set had been almost completely destroyed. The chairs were lumps of black ash and the rug was little more than a stain on the studio floor. The wood and canvas backdrop was missing altogether.

Next to the set sat the pile of old kinescopes, still smoking. The film canisters were blackened and partially melted. The wooden flat that had been used to carry them onto the set was unrecognizable.

Frank and Joe stared at the ruins of the studio in silence, then Frank whispered, "Where's the Marauder? I don't see him."

"Over there, I think," said Joe. "I saw movement of some kind."

Frank stared into the darkness, trying to make out shapes in the shadows. The ceiling of Studio A was about six feet above their heads, and the metal platform that they were standing on ran around the entire studio. At various points, other platforms—the catwalks—stretched across from one side of the studio to the other.

"There he is," Frank whispered, pointing to a dark figure standing on one of the catwalks. "He's looking down into the studio."

"Maybe he's admiring the mess he made. Wait'll I get my hands on that—"

"Shhh!" admonished Frank. "Don't let him know we're here."

"Sorry," whispered Joe. "Look, I'm going to go around the side of this platform and come at him from the other end of that catwalk. You stand over there and block his escape route. We'll trap him in the middle of the catwalk. He won't have any place to run."

"Got it!" said Frank with hushed excitement. "Let's go!"

Joe moved quickly, half walking, half crawling his way around to the far side of the studio. Frank, his eyes fixed on the dark figure on the catwalk, tiptoed to the point where the catwalk branched off from the platform that he was standing on.

The Marauder, if that's who the shadowy figure was, didn't seem to notice the Hardys. He was staring intently at the rest of the studio, studying the damage from the fire. On the far side of the figure, Frank could see Joe slowly making his way around the edge of the studio, toward the other end of the catwalk.

Frank placed a foot on the catwalk that the figure was standing on. The metal made a faint creaking sound, just enough to warn the Marauder that Frank was there. The dark figure looked up and stared into the darkness, toward the spot where Frank was crouching. Suddenly the figure stiffened.

He must have seen me! Frank thought.

The dark figure turned to run in the opposite direction. But then he saw Joe at the far end of the catwalk and froze. The three of them stood quietly for about five seconds, then the Marauder made a run for it—directly at Frank!

Frank took his best football blocking pose and waited. The Marauder ran straight into his shoulder and fell backward with a groan. The collision, however, caused the catwalk to vibrate wildly, and Frank found himself thrown against the flimsy cable that served as a guardrail, staring dizzily at the studio floor twenty feet below.

The Marauder took advantage of Frank's incapacity and, regaining his feet, jumped over Frank's unbalanced form and onto the platform beyond.

"Stop him!" yelled Joe, racing from the opposite end of the catwalk.

"I'm trying!" said Frank, struggling back to his feet.

The Marauder was heading for the door to the hallway. Frank rushed after him, catching him just before he reached the door and knocking him down onto the platform.

"I've got you!" Frank cried triumphantly, grabbing the figure by the shoulders.

"*We've* got him," corrected Joe, coming up behind the pair. Joe threw open the door to the hallway, so that they would have enough light to get a good look at the Marauder's face.

"And who exactly do you think you are?" the figure on the floor demanded gruffly. "Let go of me!"

Joe squinted at their captive. "Who is this guy?" he asked. "I've never seen him before."

Frank stared at the man's face in astonishment. "*I* have!" he said. "This is Warren Ettinger, the president of Mediatronics!"

12 The Masked Marauder ... Captured?

"That is *indeed* who I am!" the man declared. "And I would suggest that you remove your hands from me immediately, if you don't intend to spend the rest of your life in court—or in jail!"

"Not on your life, Ettinger!" protested Frank. "What were you doing up here, anyway? Admiring the damage that your little fire did to those kinescopes?"

"*My* little fire?" replied Ettinger in a baffled voice. "What in the world are you—Wait a minute! I've seen you before, haven't I? You're the young man who tried to break into the Mediatronics office yesterday. Why, you young hoodlum . . . !"

"That's great!" declared Frank. "You calling *me* a hoodlum! I overheard you telling one of your cronies that there wouldn't be 'any TV station left to sell' if WBPT didn't cooperate with your takeover scheme!"

"You were eavesdropping on me?" asked Ettinger indignantly. "Didn't your parents teach you proper manners?"

"Don't try and bluff your way out of this!" Joe interjected. "We know that you wanted to destroy those kinescopes in order to force WBPT to sell out to you!"

"Are you totally insane?" Ettinger snapped. "Why would I do anything of the sort?"

"Then what did you mean when you said there'd be no station left to sell?" said Frank. "It sounds to me as if you were going to destroy WBPT if you weren't able to buy it. Where I come from, that's known as extortion!"

"You've taken my remark completely the wrong way!" complained Ettinger. "It's undignified to explain such things to a hoodlum, but I suppose I must."

"*I'll* explain it," said a voice from the doorway. Frank and Joe turned to see Bill Amberson, the station manager, standing in the hallway, a weary look on his face.

"I heard the shouting," he told them. "I'm afraid you boys have made a mistake here. You'd better let Mr. Ettinger stand up, Frank."

"But . . . but we caught him snooping around in the studio," Frank said. "We think he had something to do with the explosion."

"I'm afraid you're a little wide of the mark," said Amberson, extending a hand to help Ettinger back to his feet.

"I have a perfect right to be in this studio," said Ettinger, dusting off his suit, "though the police officer downstairs didn't seem to think so, which is why I came up here. I practically own this place, after all. I wanted to see how severe the damage had been and whether this studio was still worth the money that I was offering for it."

"I don't understand," Frank said to Amberson. "What did he mean, then, when he said that there wouldn't be a station?"

"He meant just what he said," explained Amberson. "Without help from Mediatronics, this station would have ceased to exist years ago. I don't want you two to repeat a word of this to *anybody*, understand? WBPT has been borrowing money from Mediatronics for years. It's the only thing that's kept us afloat. And, now, we've found that we're unable to pay it back."

"Which is why," Ettinger added, "we've decided to purchase WBPT. If they can't repay the money, then the only way that we can be compensated for our loans is by purchasing the station."

"In a way," said Amberson, "they're doing us a favor. They *could* simply foreclose on the loan. The station would be theirs anyway, and the station's owners wouldn't get a cent out of the deal. By buying the station, everybody comes out ahead—except that those of us who work here will all be out of jobs."

"We're not running a charity ward!" protested Ettinger. "You should be grateful that we've

114

allowed the station to exist for this long. I'm afraid I lost my temper yesterday—when you heard me making that remark, young man. The negotiations with WBPT have been getting a little acrimonious. By 'no station left to sell,' I meant that we'd simply foreclose on the loan and be done with it. Don't think that Mediatronics hasn't been tempted to do that all along."

"Then you *weren't* threatening to blow up the station?" said Joe.

"Of course not!" said Ettinger angrily. "What sort of barbarians do you think we are?"

"Then we still don't know who the Marauder is," said Frank dismally.

"You know that it's not Mediatronics," said Amberson. "Take my word for it, Frank."

"Well," said Frank, extending his hand to Ettinger, "I apologize for tackling you."

Reluctantly, Ettinger took Frank's hand and shook it. "I suppose you were only doing what you thought right. I can't blame you for that. I think you may have knocked a few of my vertebrae out of place, however."

"Frank's a star football player," said Joe. "You're lucky it was only a few vertebrae."

Ettinger groaned. "I think I'd best be going now. We'll begin our little talks again next week, Bill. Make sure that your lawyers are present."

"I will," said Amberson in a tired voice. "You boys get on out of here," he said to the Hardys. "I'm not sure it matters anymore who the Marauder is." He turned and vanished down the stairs.

"He may not think it matters anymore," said Joe, "but *I* do! Now I want to find the Marauder more than ever!"

"I agree," said Frank. "But I'm not sure where to look next."

"Well," said Joe, "there's always Wayne Clintock. He's the other one who had a motive. Maybe we should investigate old Wayne a little more carefully."

"I don't know," said Frank. "I'm not too sure about Clintock. He—"

The stairwell door burst open and Johnny Berridge rushed out breathlessly. When he saw the Hardys, his face lit up.

"I've been looking all over for you guys!" he said excitedly. "Come on down to the engineering booth! I've got a surprise for you!"

"It's nice to see somebody around here in a good mood," said Frank. "What happened? You find another fifty episodes of 'Mrs. Brody's Boardinghouse'?"

"Even better," said Berridge. "It's those videotapes I made last night! They've turned up again!"

The director's booth was already crowded when the Hardys arrived with Johnny Berridge. Mona was there, as were Amberson, Tom

Langford, and Matt Freeman. Even Wayne Clintock was lingering in the background.

"Guess I wanted to see how this thing turned out," said Clintock. "Always like to see a criminal brought to justice. They tell me that this videotape might have a picture of the Marauder on it."

"That's right, Wayne," said Joe. "Johnny left one of his cameras running all night, so if anybody was in the studio, it'll be on the tapes."

"We've got the preliminary police report on the bombing," Mona said. "The gasoline and an incendiary bomb were hidden inside one of the spotlights on the studio ceiling. They weren't there when the bomb squad searched the studio yesterday, so the Marauder must have planted them last night or this morning. That means we should have a shot of him on the tapes."

"So where were the tapes?" Frank asked Berridge.

"I found them in a closet," said Berridge, "crammed into an old shopping bag. I guess that whoever stole them had planned to smuggle them out of the station but wasn't sure if he could get them past the cops. So he put them in the closet for later."

"Lucky you found them," said Joe.

"I've been combing the station ever since I talked to you earlier," Berridge said. "I looked in every nook and cranny I could think of."

The tapes were in big blue cartridges, much

larger than the small black cassettes used for home VCRs. Tom Langford picked up one of the cartridges and plugged it into a large tape deck on one wall of the booth. The image of Studio A appeared on the monitor, as it had looked before the fire.

"That's from last night," said Berridge.

"Looks like the studio was empty," said Frank.

"That's how most of this tape is going to look," said Langford. "Not many people hang around in Studio A in the middle of the night. I'll do a fast-forward scan through the slow part. You guys call out if you see something interesting and I'll play it through at normal speed."

Nothing happened during the entire first tape. When it ended, Langford pulled the cartridge out of the tape deck and popped the second tape in.

"I started this one at five o'clock this morning," Berridge said.

"You got in early," Frank commented.

"I usually do," Berridge said. "Besides, I wanted to put a fresh tape in the camera. I didn't want to risk having the tape run out before the Marauder appeared."

The beginning of the second tape was as dull as the last tape had been. Then, abruptly, a blurred figure darted across the studio and vanished up one of the ladders on the wall.

"There!" cried Mona. "Play that back again!"

Langford rewound the tape and played it again

118

at normal speed. This time, the viewers saw a shadowy figure emerge from the rear of the studio, a large object tucked under his arm, and climb up the ladder. A moment later, the figure reappeared on the studio floor, the large object gone. The figure glanced around the room for a moment, then disappeared through the rear door.

"The Marauder!" Berridge shouted. "It's got to be!"

"I agree," said Mona. "That thing he was carrying must have been the spotlight that contained the bomb and the gasoline. But he was too far away and the studio was too dark. I couldn't make out his face."

"I couldn't, either," said Joe. "Can we do something with that tape to make it clearer?"

Frank's eyes lit up. "Sure!" he cried. "The digital effects board! Can it be used to enhance a tape like this?" he asked Berridge.

"You bet!" cried Berridge enthusiastically. "Tom, punch up the effects board and give us a close-up of the Marauder."

"Sure," said Langford. "Let me rewind the tape again."

Within seconds, he had rewound the tape back to the point where the Marauder entered the studio. Then he punched a few buttons and brought up another copy of the image on a second monitor.

Once again, the dark figure of the Marauder

entered the studio, the deadly package tucked under his arm, and walked toward the ladder.

"Freeze it there!" said Berridge.

Langford pressed a button and the image froze, with the shadowy Marauder facing almost directly toward the camera.

"Now I'll just zoom in a bit," said Langford, turning a dial. The picture swelled in size until the image of the Marauder filled the entire screen. Unfortunately, the image was nothing more than a blurry silhouette with a few scraps of color in it.

"He's unrecognizable," said Mona disappointedly. "Is there anything you can do to bring out some detail?"

"Don't lose faith yet," said Langford. "This board can perform miracles."

He pressed another button and a ripple passed across the image of the Marauder. The blurred edges of the silhouette became sharper and the scraps of color became clearer.

"That's better," said Frank, "but we still can't tell who it is."

"Give it a minute," said Langford as another ripple passed across the screen. "This may take a little work, but I think the board can handle it."

A third ripple passed across the screen, and the object that the Marauder was holding became clearly visible.

"It's a spotlight, all right," said Mona. "That's the bomb. We've got our man!"

"If we can only recognize him," said Joe.

Another ripple passed across the screen. The Marauder's face started to appear.

"I can make out his eyes and nose!" said Berridge. "Anybody recognize him?"

"Not yet," said Mona. "Stay calm, Johnny."

After a fifth ripple passed across the screen, the Marauder's mouth and chin became visible.

"He *does* look familiar!" said Mona. "I . . . I think I know who that is!"

Yet another ripple passed across the image of the Marauder. Now the face was so clear that everybody in the room knew who they were looking at.

Wayne Clintock!

13 The Lady Vanishes

Pandemonium filled the director's booth.

"That's not possible!" cried Clintock. "I wasn't even in your building this morning!"

"I don't get it," said Berridge in a baffled voice. "Why would he—Clintock—want to destroy the studio?"

"It was the kinescopes, wasn't it?" said Amberson, casting a furious look in Clintock's direction. "You set this whole thing up just to destroy the kinescopes, didn't you?"

Clintock stood stiffly against the rear wall of the booth, a stunned look on his face. "I had nothing to do with this," he said finally, his western drawl almost totally gone. "I'd never do anything like this. You know that!"

"That's not what the tape shows!" Amberson replied. "Pictures don't lie, Clintock. We've got the evidence against you. It's not much of a

122

satisfaction after all that's happened, but, with that tape, we'll be able to send you to prison."

"Prison?" said Clintock. "But I haven't done anything! You've got to believe me!"

"Get the police, Mona," said Amberson. "We'll show them the tape and have Clintock arrested."

"You . . . you can't!" Clintock stammered, as Mona left the booth.

"I'm afraid we can," said Amberson. "Your career is over, Clintock. I can't believe you'd do something like this just to save your macho reputation."

"But . . . but . . ." Clintock sputtered, at a loss for a reply.

A few minutes later, Mona returned with a pair of police officers in tow. Langford played the videotape again, showing the police the pictures of the Marauder entering the studio, then enhancing the images to reveal Clintock's face. Then one of the officers put handcuffs on Clintock's wrists and led him away, while Clintock protested loudly.

"Well," said Mona, as they filed out of the booth. "It's over now. It's too late to save the kinescopes or the station, of course, but at least the Masked Marauder has been caught."

"I guess you won't be needing us anymore," said Joe.

"On the contrary," said Mona. "I still want you

to do your Crimestoppers spot on 'Faces and Places,' at least for the rest of the week. If it goes well and we get a good reaction, I'd like to keep you on as regulars."

"Well, it might interfere with school," said Joe. "But we'll think about it." He turned to Frank. "What's wrong with you? You don't look very excited. We just solved a case, didn't we?"

"There's something wrong here," said Frank. "I'm not so sure that Clintock was really the Marauder."

"What are you talking about?" said Joe. "You saw that videotape. Wayne Clintock was carrying the bomb, clear as day. What more do you want?"

"I don't know," said Frank. "Something just doesn't seem right, but I can't put my finger on it." He looked at Mona. "Do you still have that last tape that the Marauder sent you? The one where he threatened to attack the station a second time?"

"Sure," Mona said. "It's in my office. Why?"

"Do you think Tom Langford could enhance that tape with his digital effects board?" asked Frank.

"I suppose so. But what good would it do?"

"I'm not sure," said Frank. "Call it a hunch. The Marauder used some sort of electronic technique on that tape to make his voice unrecognizable. Maybe Langford can reprocess the voice with his effects board and we can match it against Clintock's, to see if it sounds like him."

124

"Not a bad idea," said Mona. "Wait here. I'll get the tape."

Mona returned from her office a few minutes later with the small tape cassette containing the message from the Marauder. Moments later, they had tracked down Langford and returned to the director's booth. The engineer placed the tape cassette in a smaller tape deck just below the one where he had played the tape that Berridge's camera had made.

"Watch the monitor," said Langford. "Here's our friend the Marauder again."

The Marauder's masked face appeared on the screen, his electronically altered voice delivering the message that they had first heard the previous day.

"Can you process his voice with that thing?" Frank asked. "So that we can find out what the Marauder really sounds like?"

"I think so," said Langford, "though most of my experience has been in image processing. I'm not so sure how successful I'll be with sounds, but I'll give it a try. It might not come out as well as that picture of Clintock's face did."

He turned a few knobs, and the Marauder's voice shot up and down the scale, from low-pitched to high-pitched back to low-pitched again. Then he punched a button and the voice became less electronic, more human-sounding.

"That's better," said Joe. "It almost sounds familiar. It doesn't sound like Clintock, either."

"No, it doesn't," said Mona. "Can you make it sound a little more natural, Tom?"

"Sorry," said Langford. "That's the best I can manage."

"What's that noise in the background?" asked Frank. "Do you hear it?"

"Yeah," said Joe. "Kind of a high-pitched noise, like radio static."

"It's probably a side effect of the sound processing I just did," said Langford. "Don't worry about it. I doubt that it's important."

"No," said Mona. "I recognize that sound. I've heard it someplace before . . . but I don't remember where."

"Well," said Frank, "it was worth trying. Thanks, Tom. I wish we'd gotten better results, but it's not your fault. I guess Joe and I had better get home now."

"Thanks for your help, guys," said Mona. "I'll expect you in here bright and early tomorrow morning to work on 'Faces and Places.' And if I remember where I've heard that sound before, I'll let you know."

The next morning the Hardys were at the breakfast table shortly before eight A.M., devouring Aunt Gertrude's ham and eggs.

"So what's this feeling you've got that Clintock isn't the Marauder?" Joe asked Frank. "Just a hunch? Or do you have some solid evidence?"

"I'm not sure," Frank said. "I think it has something to do with electronics. Whoever the Marauder is, he's obviously an electronics expert. Remember that remote control device he put on the camera crane? And the way he patched the VCR into the WBPT transmitter?"

"Sure," agreed Joe, "and the way he electronically altered his voice on the tape. Obviously the guy knew what he was doing. So what's the problem? Don't you think Clintock could have done that?"

"No," said Frank. "I don't. I read something about Clintock a couple of years ago that said he got into acting because he didn't know how to do anything else. I mean, he didn't have other talents or skills. Then, in high school, he discovered that he could act. And the rest is history."

"Maybe he's been taking a correspondence-school course in electronics," said Joe.

"Why? He's extremely successful at what he does. He's one of the richest actors in the world. Why would he want to get into electronics?"

"Maybe he got somebody else to do that part for him."

"I don't buy that," said Frank. "I think Clintock would have taken an easier route, like sending written messages instead of videotapes. All of this electronic stuff just doesn't sound like Clintock's style to me."

"Okay," said Joe agreeably. "Let's say that the

Marauder is an electronics expert. What does that—"

"Hey," Frank interrupted. "The light's flashing on the answering machine. Did you hear the phone ring?"

"No," said Joe. "It must have happened before we woke up. But who would be calling that early?"

Frank walked over to the machine, rewound the tape, then punched the playback button. After a few seconds a message began to chatter out of the tiny speaker.

"Frank? Joe?" said Mona D'Angelo's voice. "You've got to meet me at the studio as soon as possible. I've found proof that Wayne Clintock is *not* the Masked Marauder! And I think I . . . Oh!" Her voice cut off abruptly. There was a series of thumping noises, as though the phone had dropped to the floor, then the sound of the receiver slamming violently back into the cradle.

Frank gave Joe a stunned look.

"Something's wrong," he said. "We'd better get to the studio—fast!"

The brothers pulled into the TV station parking lot twenty minutes later, parked, and sprinted up the front walk. When they arrived at Mona's office, however, the producer was nowhere to be found.

"Just what I was afraid of!" said Frank. "She's gone."

"Look at this office!" Joe said. "Papers all over

128

the place. It looks like there's been some sort of struggle in here."

"You're right," said Frank. "It does."

"You know what this means, don't you?" asked Joe.

"Right," said Frank. "Something's happened to Mona—and I'll bet it's nothing good."

14 Search Party

"You're sure this isn't a joke of some kind?" Sergeant Con Riley asked Frank and Joe as they stood in Mona's office. "We've already got that Marauder fellow—Wayne Clintock—in jail. Who else would have wanted to kidnap Ms. D'Angelo?"

"We don't know," said Joe.

"Well," said Con, "nobody can find her around the station, and she doesn't answer her home phone. You're sure you had a message from her this morning?"

"Yes," said Frank, for the hundredth time.

"And she said something about knowing who the Marauder *really* is?" Con asked him dubiously.

"Yes," repeated Frank.

"Okay." The police officer shrugged. "We'll do our best to find her, but I don't think we're

130

going to let this Clintock guy out of jail quite yet. If you guys hear from her again, get in touch with us right away. Understand?"

"We will," said Joe. "Thanks."

As Con left the office, Johnny Berridge appeared at the door. "There you are," he said. "I've been looking all over for you."

"Did you hear what happened to Mona?" Frank asked.

"Yes," said Berridge. "One of the cops in the hallway told me. It's terrible. Who do you think could have been responsible?"

"The Marauder," said Frank. "Who else?"

Berridge looked puzzled. "But we've already caught the Marauder."

"I'm not so sure about that," said Frank.

"So why were you looking for us?" asked Joe.

"It's time to start working on your Crimestoppers spot, the one for this afternoon's show."

The brothers stared at Berridge as though he had gone crazy. "After Mona's been kidnapped? You guys don't stop for anything, do you?"

"As Mona always says, 'The show must go on,'" quoted Berridge. "I'm sure it's what she wants us to do."

Berridge led the Hardys to the equipment room, where he grabbed a hand-held camera and the brothers put together a few props to use in their presentation at the Waterview Apartments.

131

While they were rummaging through the shelves, Tom Langford poked his head in the door to say hello.

"Got some spare time?" Berridge asked Langford. "We'll need some help with this remote broadcast. I'd appreciate it if you could come along."

"Sure," said Langford. "We just wrapped the morning news. I can get somebody else to handle lights in Studio B for 'Faces and Places.' Be with you in a minute."

Fifteen minutes later, Frank, Joe, Berridge, and Langford were standing in the parking lot. Berridge looked around with a puzzled expression on his face.

"Where's the mobile van?" he asked. "It was right out here yesterday afternoon."

"Somebody else must be using it," Langford said. "We can use the backup van. I've got the keys."

The backup van was a slightly smaller version of the mobile van that Berridge had shown Frank and Joe the day before. Berridge opened the rear door and Frank and Joe threw their props into the back of the van. Then Joe and Langford climbed into the rear and Frank and Berridge took a seat up front. Frank had to shift to avoid sitting on Berridge's camera.

"Why didn't you toss this in the back?" Frank asked.

Berridge grinned. "Never go anywhere without my camera. You never know when you might run across a great shot." He put the key in the ignition and started the engine.

Frank sat up straight, suddenly alert.

"Something wrong?" Berridge asked.

"I'm not sure," Frank said. "Something sounds strange. That high-pitched noise—what is it?"

"Oh," said Berridge. "That's just some of the electronic equipment in the back of the van. It always makes that noise. Why?"

"That's the sound that we heard on the Marauder's tape last night," said Frank. "Tom Langford processed the tape for us with the digital effects board and we heard this noise in the background. Mona said that it sounded familiar. This must be where she'd heard it before."

"Could be," said Berridge. "Mona's been in the van plenty of times."

"Then that means the Marauder must have used the van to make his tapes," said Frank. "Do you have equipment in here for making cassette tapes?"

"No," said Berridge. "We've got the equipment for making large cartridge tapes, like I use in the studio, but not the small cassette ones that the Marauder used."

"What about the other van?" asked Frank. "The one that wasn't in the parking lot. Does it have the equipment?"

Berridge thought for a moment. "Yes. It does. The newspeople like to work with the smaller cassettes occasionally, so they can take them home and play them on their VCRs."

"Then the Marauder could have used the other van to make his cassettes!" said Frank excitedly.

"That's possible," said Berridge. "But what good does it do us to know that?"

"Can you find out who has the other van?" asked Frank. "I've got a hunch that if we can find that other van, it may lead us to the Marauder."

"Shouldn't be a problem to find out," Berridge said. "Hang on. I'll talk to the front desk."

Berridge pulled a small microphone from the seat beside him and punched a button on a CB radio underneath the dashboard.

"Marge," he said into the microphone. "This is Johnny Berridge in the backup van. Can you tell me who signed out the remote van this morning?"

"Sure," said a voice on the radio. "Hang on a minute." A moment later, the voice returned and said, "Says here that Mona D'Angelo signed it out, at six-thirty this morning. That was before I got here. The night guard must have given her the keys."

"Thanks, Marge," said Berridge. "Talk to you later."

"That's probably about the time Mona left the message on our answering machine," said Frank. "But why would she have taken the van?"

"I don't know," said Berridge. "I have to admit, that sounds pretty strange."

"Is there a way to track down the other van?" asked Frank. "Does it send out any kind of radio signal that we can pick up?"

"Depends on whether the carrier wave's switched on," said Berridge. "If it is, we can pick up the signal on the radio in this van and follow it like a homing device. Here. Let's try it."

Berridge threw a switch on the CB radio and turned the knob briskly. A faint humming noise filled the cab of the van.

"That's it!" said Berridge. "The carrier wave! Let's follow it!"

Frank leaned between the seats and yelled around the metal partition that separated them from the rear of the van, where Joe and Langford were sitting: "We're going to make a slight detour! I'll explain later!"

Berridge pulled the van out of the parking lot and into the street. For a few minutes the signal on the radio grew stronger, then it began to fade.

"We must have made a wrong turn!" said Berridge. He turned the van around and went back about two blocks, then turned west. The signal began growing stronger again.

They tracked the signal for about half an hour, backtracking every time they started to lose it. Finally, the road they were following came to a dead end.

"That's the only way left to go," said Frank, pointing at a faint dirt trail that led into the woods.

"Can't hurt to try it," said Berridge, guiding the van off the road and onto the trail. As they bumped along the dirt road, the carrier wave signal grew increasingly louder, until it sounded as if they must be right on top of the source. The dirt trail ended abruptly at a grove of trees.

"We can't go any farther," said Berridge. "What now?"

"Let's get out and look around," suggested Frank.

He opened the door of the van and dropped to the ground. Berridge climbed out the other side, then opened the rear door to let Joe and Langford out.

"We think Mona's around here somewhere," Frank explained, "in the other remote van. You guys look over there, Johnny and I will search in this direction."

The spot where they had parked was surrounded by thick shrubbery, trees, and ground cover. The smell of honeysuckle filled the air.

"What's that over there?" cried Joe, pointing to a metallic glint behind some bushes.

Berridge grabbed a handful of branches and pulled them aside. "It's the van, all right!" he cried.

The four of them worked for a few minutes to unbury the van from where it had been concealed in the bushes. Once the vegetation had been cleared away, Berridge reached up to open the rear door.

"Wait a minute!" said Frank. "Are you sure it's safe?"

"As sure as I'll ever be," said Berridge. "Why wouldn't it be safe?"

"The Marauder might still be around here," Frank said. "Grab the door from one side, open it, then drop back into the trees."

Berridge did as Frank asked, while the others moved a safe distance away from the van. At Berridge's urging, one of the two rear doors popped open and swung gently in the wind. There was only darkness inside.

Joe and Frank crept up carefully behind the van, opening the other door and peering inside.

"There's someone in there!" Joe said.

"It's Mona!" cried Frank.

Mona D'Angelo, bound and gagged and lying on the floor of the van, looked up at the Hardys with wide eyes.

"I think she's okay!" Joe said. "Frank, help me cut these ropes off her!"

Berridge climbed into the rear of the van after the Hardys. "What's this stuff back here?" he asked, pointing to a tarpaulin covering a large pile of something in the rear of the van, behind Mona.

"I don't know," said Joe. "Why don't you take a look while we get Mona untied?"

Berridge pulled the tarpaulin away and dropped it on the floor of the van. Underneath was a familiar-looking stack of blue film canisters.

"I don't believe it!" he exclaimed. "It's the kinescopes! The episodes of 'Mrs. Brody's Boardinghouse!'"

"What?" cried Joe. "But those were burned up in the fire! I saw them burn with my own eyes!"

Frank pulled the gag from Mona's mouth. She gasped for a moment, then her eyes darted toward the open rear door of the van.

"Joe!" she shouted. "Frank! Look out! Look behind you!"

Joe and Frank turned to see a dark figure in the rear door. It was Tom Langford, pointing a gun directly at them.

"Everybody stay calm," he said coolly. "Sit down and behave yourselves. We're about to take a little drive, just the five of us."

15 The Marauder's Last Stand

"What are you doing, Tom?" exclaimed Berridge. "I . . . I don't understand!"

"Sorry, Johnny," said Langford. "Nothing personal. I'd hoped to keep all of you out of this, but these guys are a little too smart for their own good. Now I want you all to do what I just asked you to do: sit down and behave. Don't make me ask you again, okay?"

He waved the gun threateningly. Reluctantly, Frank and Berridge sat down on the hard metal floor. Joe sat across from them beside Mona. Langford entered the van and had them tie one another up tightly with insulated electric wiring.

"What are you going to do now?" Joe asked. "Leave us here?"

"Hardly," said Langford. "I'd just as soon be done with all of you right now, but I can't afford the luxury. I'm going to take a little trip with the

139

four of you as my passengers. We'll talk again in a minute."

Langford walked to the rear of the van and jumped to the ground, then closed the doors and bolted them shut. A moment later, they heard him climb into the driver's seat and gun the van's engines. After a couple of minutes, the van started moving.

"I'm sorry I had to get you all into this," said Mona. "I thought when I turned on the carrier wave signal that it might lead you to me, but I never dreamed that you'd bring *him* along."

"That was my fault," said Berridge. "Who would have suspected Tom Langford? He's always seemed like a nice enough guy."

"*We* should have suspected him." Frank sighed. "It fits. The Marauder had to be an electronics expert, and Langford is the head electronics engineer at WBPT. I should have figured that out."

"So what happened?" Joe asked Mona. "How did you wind up here?"

"I had trouble sleeping last night. I guess everything that happened yesterday had gotten me wired up, and I kept remembering what Frank said about Clintock maybe not being the Marauder. So I tried to remember where I'd heard that high-pitched noise on the tape before. About five-thirty this morning, I remembered. It was in this van."

140

"Yeah," said Frank. "We figured that out, too, only it was a little late."

"I raced to the station as soon as I remembered. When I looked inside the van, I found that stack of kinescopes, and I knew that Clintock couldn't possibly have put them there. That narrowed down the list of suspects considerably. That's when I telephoned you. Unfortunately, Langford had seen me snooping around. He caught up with me as I was speaking on the phone in my office. Then he forced me at gunpoint to sign out the mobile van. He shoved me in the back of the van, tied me up, and drove out here into the woods and left me here. I think he was planning to come back later and . . . and take care of me."

"Good thing we found you, then," said Joe.

"Oh, yeah," said Frank, "a lot of good this is doing her."

"Hey, we're not down for the count yet!" declared Joe. "Where's that old detective spirit? Don't you have a plan yet for getting us out of here?"

"As a matter of fact, I think I might," said Frank. "Johnny, can Langford hear what we say back here?"

"No," said Berridge. "The metal partition's in the way, and the engine drowns out conversation from the rear."

"Good," said Frank. "We can talk freely. How do you turn on the transmitter in this van?"

"There's a switch about six inches above my head," the cameraman replied.

"Think you can reach it?" asked Frank.

"Not with my hands tied," said Berridge. "I might be able to reach it with my head . . . if I were six inches taller."

"Here," said Joe, stretching his feet out to where Berridge was seated on the opposite side of the van. "Press your feet against mine and I'll push."

Berridge did as Joe asked. The younger Hardy pushed the cameraman against the wall, so that Berridge could work his way upward toward the transmitter switch.

"There!" cried Berridge, bumping the switch with the top of his head. "Got it! Now what?"

"Okay," said Frank. "Now help me figure out how to loosen up these wires around my wrists. . . ."

Ten minutes later the van came to a halt. Langford opened the doors at the rear, and bright sunlight streamed into the dark compartment where his four captives were seated. The van was parked on a narrow dirt road not unlike the one where they had found Mona. Not far away they could see a high-rise apartment building.

"We're at the Waterview Apartments!" said Frank in a surprised tone. "This is where we were going to do our Crimestoppers spot!"

"That's right, Frank," said Langford. "But I'm

afraid you're not going to have the chance to film that spot."

"What are you going to do to us?"

"Each of you gets a little love tap from the butt of this gun," Langford said, holding out the weapon. "Just enough to knock you out while I untie you and push this van into Barmet Bay."

"Barmet Bay?" exclaimed Joe. "Have you gone completely wacko?"

"The Waterview Apartments are located practically on top of the famous Barmet Cliffs," said Langford, "overlooking Bayport's beautiful Barmet Bay. It'll look as though you had an unfortunate accident while filming your remote demonstration. Somebody drove just a little too close to the cliffs, maybe to get a pretty location shot, and the van went into the water with all of its occupants inside. Alas, there were no survivors."

"We're pretty good swimmers," said Joe.

"That'll do us a lot of good when we're unconscious," said Frank sourly.

"So why did you do it, Tom?" asked Joe. "You were after the kinescopes, right?"

"That's right," said Langford. "There are some people who believe that the revival of 'Mrs. Brody's Boardinghouse' is going to be the hottest thing on television in years. A station in Boston has offered me half a million dollars for those kinescopes—strictly under the table, of course."

"Won't it look a little suspicious when the

143

kinescopes that supposedly burned up in Bayport turn up in one piece in Boston?" asked Frank.

"Why?" said Langford. "Anybody with a movie camera and a television set could have made a kinescope back in the fifties. There's no way to know whether other kinescopes of 'Mrs. Brody's Boardinghouse' exist. And they're in the public domain. When the original copyright ran out back in the seventies, WBPT didn't renew their rights because they didn't know then that any copies existed. So when these turn up in Boston, it'll be announced that a second cache of kinescopes has been discovered. How fortunate! The world won't have to be deprived of this classic television show for another terrible moment!"

"But we saw the kinescopes burn up!" said Joe. "We were standing right next to them!"

"Fortunately," said Langford, "the film canisters that you saw burn up in the fire contained nothing but old commercials and soap operas. I put the *real* kinescopes in the van for safekeeping —right after I gimmicked the sprinkler system to make sure it was completely destroyed. I'd have sold 'Mrs. Brody's Boardinghouse' in Boston this afternoon, if it hadn't been for the nosy Ms. D'Angelo here."

"What about that tape showing Wayne Clintock planting the bomb?" asked Frank. "You stole the tapes and added that yourself, right?"

"Right," said Langford agreeably. "You wouldn't believe how easy it is to fake a tape like

144

that using the digital effects board. If only that skinflint Amberson had known what he was getting into when he bought that board! I've never liked the old buzzard, anyway. Serves him right. And Clintock is an arrogant son of a gun, like all movie stars. I can't feel sorry for him, either. All I did was take a scene from one of his old movies and chroma-key in a picture of Studio A in place of the background. Then I pasted the picture of the spotlight into his arms and I had all the incriminating evidence that I needed."

"I should have stuck to it when I said I'd never believe anything that I saw on television again!" cried Joe. "I didn't know how right I was!"

"What I don't understand," said Frank, "is how you managed to blow yourself up that first day in the studio, when Joe saved your life. Did you do that just so you wouldn't look suspicious?"

Langford seemed to blush slightly. "That was an accident," he replied reluctantly. "I'd forgotten about Murphy's Law. Anything that can go wrong, will. I'd already planted the bomb in one of the spots, and I accidentally triggered it while adjusting the lights."

"Was it really a dud, like the police said?"

Langford laughed. "No. It was actually a very small bomb. It wasn't supposed to blow up the studio, just establish the existence of an outside threat. And it worked better than I expected. Since I was the only one put in real danger, no one ever suspected that I was the Marauder. I could switch the kinescopes and set fire to the station anytime. Once the format for Wednesday's show was set it was all so easy. I just rigged up my fire bomb on Tuesday night and made the kinescope switch. As I said, it was easy.

"I'd like to stand around and chat with you guys," Langford went on, "but we've got to get this over with. If we hang around back here too long, somebody from those apartments might get suspicious and come over to check out the action. I'll try to make this as painless as possible—"

Suddenly Langford's eyes narrowed. Sitting next to Johnny Berridge in the back of the van was Berridge's hand-held TV camera. Next to the lens, the tiny red light was glowing.

"You fool!" said Langford. "You left your camera on! Are you making a tape of me? A fat lot of good that's going to do you! I'll just erase it before I dump you in the bay!"

"It's not a tape," said Frank. "We're broadcasting a live feed back to WBPT. Look over there." Frank nodded toward the nearby apartment building.

Langford turned automatically in the direction that Frank was facing. Through the window of a ground floor apartment, he could see a large projection-screen television. On the screen was the profile of a man's face.

His own face.

"Faces and Places" was on the air—live!

146

16 Caught in the Act

Langford stumbled backward, as though someone had punched him in the stomach. Frank Hardy, shaking off the bonds that he had been loosening while Langford was talking, leaped out of the back of the van and tackled Langford around the waist. The gun flew out of Langford's hand and landed in the grass nearby.

The engineer was stronger than Frank would have guessed, however. He punched Frank in the jaw hard enough to knock him to one side and turned to crawl in the direction of the gun.

"No, you don't!" Frank shouted, stumbling after him. He grabbed Langford under the arms and pulled him back to his feet. Langford responded by kicking Frank sharply in the shins.

Langford dived for the gun, but Frank landed on top of him a split second later. He grabbed the gun from Langford's hands before the engineer could get a tight grip and, with his best football-passing technique, tossed it high in the air. It vanished into the bushes.

Langford, meanwhile, scrambled back to his feet and started running again. Joe Hardy, having finally loosened his own bonds, leaped out of the back of the van.

"Stop him!" Joe yelled. "He's trying to get away!"

Frank rose awkwardly to his feet. "Where's he going to go?" he said with a smile. "There's no place he can run to."

Even as Frank was speaking, the sound of a police siren filled the air. Three squad cars squealed around the corner next to the apartment building and braked to a halt in front of Langford. The engineer stood frozen, then threw up his hands quickly when he found himself facing six police revolvers.

"Hold it right there!" shouted one of the police officers.

"He's not armed," said Frank. "His gun's over there in the woods some place."

One of the police officers handcuffed Langford and put him in the backseat of a squad car. Con Riley got out from behind the wheel, shaking his head.

"This is the most amazing thing I've ever seen!" he muttered.

"Good to see you, Con," said Joe. "You guys just happen to be driving by here?"

148

"You kidding?" said Con Riley, a dazed look on his face. "We were just sitting around the squad room, playing cards. Then somebody suggested we turn on his favorite TV show, 'Faces and Places.'"

Frank laughed. "Bet you never dreamed that you'd be *part* of the show, did you?" He turned and nodded toward Johnny Berridge, who was walking toward them with his hand-held camera pointed in their direction. The red light next to the lens glowed brightly.

"Say hello to the guys back in the squad room, Con," Frank laughed.

"I apologize if I was a little tough on you boys," said Amberson, lounging behind his oversize desk, an uncharacteristic smile on his face. "I can't thank you enough for getting those kinescopes back for us. Now we'll have the money to pay back the loan to Mediatronics and they won't be buying us out after all. We'll be keeping old Angus's station in the McParton family."

Mona nodded in agreement. "I want to thank you, too . . . and not just for the kinescopes. Ever since Joe saved Langford's life on the air Monday, the overnight ratings for 'Faces and Places' have soared."

"It's my brother's star quality," Frank said, patting Joe on the back. "He's been telling me all about it. He's expecting a call from a big Hollywood studio at any minute."

149

"I don't know why they're taking so long," said Joe. "I hope Aunt Gertrude remembers to take their messages."

"Of course," said Frank, "that fire on the air Wednesday probably helped your ratings, too."

"Not to mention all that excitement with Langford yesterday," said Joe.

"True," said Mona. "This week, at least, 'Faces and Places' has been the most exciting show on the air. We're on the front page of all the papers."

"Then I guess you don't need us any more. Crimestoppers, Inc., is going to look pretty unexciting compared with the big-time celebrities you'll probably have on the show now."

"Wait a minute!" said Mona, laughing. "I fully expect you boys to be back with Crimestoppers, Inc., next week!"

"We'll be back if you want us," Joe said. "And if Johnny Berridge can be convinced it's safe to go back into the studio with the Hardy Boys."

"He can be convinced," said Mona. "We've given him a raise in salary. He did save my life, after all—with your help, of course."

"Then we'll see you Monday," Frank said to Mona. The brothers shook hands with Mona and Amberson, then walked into the hallway.

"So," said Joe, "it looks like the Masked Marauder is out of the picture. We can concentrate on being TV stars now."

"You be the TV star," said Frank. "I guess I just

don't have your charisma. And two stars in one family would be too much anyway."

"Uh-oh," said Joe, looking through the glass front doors of the building. A crowd of adolescent girls was standing on the front steps, autograph books at the ready. "Looks like the Joe Hardy Fan Club is here. Well, I can't keep my public waiting. . . ."

As Joe and Frank stepped through the front door, a squeal of delight went up from the crowd of young girls, and they instantly surrounded the Hardys.

"Aren't you Frank Hardy?" one of them asked.

"Yeah, we saw you on TV yesterday!" said another.

"It was so brave the way you got that gun away from that guy!" said a third.

"Can I have your autograph?" asked the first.

"Uh, sure," said Frank, a startled look on his face.

"Hey!" cried Joe. "Don't you want *my* autograph?"

"Who are you?" said the first girl.

"We want *Frank's* autograph!" said the second, with a sigh.

Frank gave Joe a shrug and began signing autographs. "What was I saying about *two* stars in one family?" He laughed.

"Maybe I wasn't cut out for television after all." Joe sighed, and settled down on the steps for a long wait.